RETURN TO STANLEY CANYON

GLENN COLEMAN

Printed in the United States of America
ISBN:1-4392-5315-3
EAN13: 9781439253151
Visit www.booksurge.com to order additional copies.

Acknowledgement

I am certain that there must be authors out there who are disciplined enough to write regularly and consistently. I must not be one of them. Even though I love to tell a good story, I depend on my family and my friends to shame me back into the office to <u>git back to writing</u>! I cannot say that I'd rather be working on my old cars or my electric trains. I cannot say that I'd rather be playing with my wonderful grandkids. I cannot say that I'd rather be tinkering out in my shop. I do love to write, but I need the constant jabbing to keep on track. Thanks to each of you who keeps asking about how the book is coming. I am getting better.

And to the girl next door, Courtney, who already has a couple of romance novels under her belt, thanks. When I have been tardy in my writing, I avoid her at all costs. I know she will stick the writing knife in my heart. She will smile beautifully and ask the words I do not want to hear. "How's the book coming?"

A special thanks must go to my editors, Jan Wiggins and Craig Scott. Just when I think I have written the next best seller, they appropriately and gently bring me back to a soft landing with their comments and suggestions. Likewise, when I cannot capture the thought process of a particular character in a story, thanks to those who lead me there. I never hesitate to ask, and so many of my friends give me excellent advice.

And to my Mom, thanks for sending my letters from college back and corrected with your red pen. Once an English teacher, always an English teacher.

Now to the real "Pete" and "Dave"…men with real hearts, true courage, Spartan dreams, and bullet-proof character. I have been blessed with your friendships.

And finally to Charlie Stebbins, my upperclassman at the Air Force Academy. This book was written to tell him "thanks" for helping me grow up and for helping me through my life. He will always be on my short list of good men. One never knows the influence, good or bad, one holds on another. He wasn't as mean as Stebinski in this book, but…

Enjoy the story,

Glenn Coleman

1

The winds howl incessantly down through Stanley
Canyon. Legend has it that the Indians refused to
live in Pine Valley below because of those winds. That
legend tells of how an entire village was destroyed by
the winds and the ensuing blizzard one freezing night
many years ago along the Front Range of the Colorado
Rockies. When the mind is still and the spirit receptive,
you can still feel the pain suffered and hear the
muffled tears of that night. They still live in the wind's
howling refrain.

Whether spirits really exist is a moot point when
you enter the peaceful magnitude and solace of the
mountains, miles and years from your other life. You
become part of nature, reduced to the same common
denominator as the mountain lion, squirrel and
pine tree. The rules and the game board are entirely
different, and you are no longer in control. You walk
among giants, you smell the ozone of the lightning,
you grovel in the dust from whence you came. You are
an insignificant pawn in God's laws of nature...yet the
only reason they exist or even matter.

You feel about you a presence so close that you want to address them, yet out of fear and reverence, you do not. When you walk the mountains, the spirits are there, perhaps only in your heart and mind, but they are there. Be still and listen, and over the pounding of your heart, you will hear them welcoming you to their haven. Enter as friend, but only as a niche in the edifice of history.

It was in that spirit that Dave came back up into the high canyon that snowy evening. His loneliness tightened his chest, and even with the exertion of the climb, his breaths were short and shallow. Pete had been his best friend since their first day as Air Force Academy cadets almost seven years earlier. Their trip together was about to end. His mission tonight was to return spirit to spirit, dust to dust.

The trail was steep and the rocks slippery from the snow and ice, but he had experienced worse many times in this canyon, and his calling again was higher than the challenge. As he reached the wide part of the trail where it turns back to the west, where others had built a small stone wall as a resting place for weary climbers, Dave took off his backpack, placed it on the wall, and slumped down in the snow at the base of the wall. His uncle had brought that old backpack from WWII. It was just an old worn-out canvas backpack with a draw string made from parachute shroud line at the top. Sewn to the khaki cover was a patch of a bulldog wearing an old-style WWI helmet. Dave had never thought to ask his uncle what the patch stood for, but Dave and his backpack had covered many trails and most of Dave's life together.

The canyon above was narrow and the winds coming down especially strong on this cold night. The icy waters tumbling over and through the boulders of the canyon coupled with the howling of the wind created majestic music that only those of the mountains have experienced and truly appreciate.

Many times had Dave and Pete sat together on that stone wall, throwing rocks into the canyon and resting before the final trek on up the mountain to the beaver pond at the head of the canyon. The fishing was always good up there and the stresses distant. Many times had they shared their hopes and fears, ambitions and frailties. Getting through the rigors of the Air Force Academy, just north of Stanley Canyon, had not been easy for either of them...but it is never easy for those who challenge its challenge, who continually raise the bar. Dave may have always been stronger and tougher than Pete, but that never seemed to matter to either of them. Pete had always been the more stable of the two roommates, cooler in stress and wiser in response. Good friends willingly share their strengths and, without reason or expectation, cover each other's flank. Though cut from different bolts of cloth, the threads that wove them together created strength and an undying love. One plus one once again equals three.

* * *

2

As a high school kid, Pete Benedetto had endured about all he could of South Philly…the crowded neighborhoods, the poverty, the polluted air, the constant inherent bickering of a large, too-close Italian family. He was the oldest of six children, and more responsibility fell on his shoulders than he thought should have.

The Benedettos lived in a walk-up just north of Veterans Stadium and the Naval Shipyard. His old man worked as a welder at the shipyard and had tried to convince Pete to join him there. He said it was a good clean living, but Pete soon learned there was nothing clean about it. Pete learned how to lay down a good bead with a stick welder and had even joined the union…but in the back of his mind, he sought only one thing…a one-way ticket out of Philadelphia.

Pete thought a lot about the future. He knew that he didn't know or have a destination…just a journey. And he was anxious and ready for that part of his life to get underway. He loved to read Thomas Wolfe and Mark Twain and Zane Grey and their adventures from the Western frontier. There was an unknown magic, or perhaps just illusion, about those lives and times. He often wondered if perhaps in another life he had lived west of the Mississippi…a strange thought for a kid raised in a Catholic school. His talent for writing short stories and poetry reflected that love and attraction. Pete's old man harassed him continuously for his love of the letters, claiming that that sort of behavior was only for the effeminate. The battle raged within Pete as to which master to serve…the Spartan warrior or the Renaissance man. This was a battle that Pete openly acknowledged, enjoyed and honored…never anxious for a victory or a retreat. He humored his old man and kept his thoughts and his writings to himself. To write is to expose yourself to your audience. While most keep those private thoughts, emotions and fears under wrap, the writer and poet lay it all out on the table for others to dissect and critique. He had shared several of his works with his priest, but for the most part, Pete kept his writings and his passions for his own pleasure.

Pete figured he had two things going for him. He was smart and would finish near the top of his high school class. Maybe there was some scholarship money out there somewhere to get him into a decent college… somewhere out of state. He knew that if he could just get in, he would do well. Pete knew his strengths and how to apply them. He was driven to succeed in whatever he chose, and college would be no different.

The other thing Pete had was good athletic ability. He loved sports and loved to compete even more. There

was something about competing that made his blood
flow warmer, and he didn't appreciate losing or losers.
To hell with the lessons learned in a loss. Whether it
was a pick-up basketball game at the Rec Center or a
lacrosse match down on the fields near the Delaware
River, Pete was going to be there. He loved the contact
sports, and the taste of his own blood in his mouth
took his game to the next level. He was selected as an
All-State Point Defenseman his junior year, a tough
feat in a lacrosse-minded state. If you came in for a
shot at the crease, you'd pay dearly if Pete were on
the field. Pete was never the fastest kid on the field,
and this led him to a life-long philosophy…"If I can't
run the fastest, then I'll run the longest." He stayed in
good shape and finished each match at the same speed
and vigor and intensity as when he started.

His mind and his body were to serve as his ticket out
of town. He had little plan past that, but knew that
was enough. One of Pete's strongest assets was that
he knew what he knew…and he knew what he didn't
know…but never feared it…only respected it. He was
confident that, given enough time, he could master
any challenge. His life would start again the moment
he saw Philly disappear below the horizon in the rear-
view mirror. It wasn't a matter of if, but when.

On a cold day just before Christmas of his senior year,
a Marine recruiter came to his high school. "Maybe,
just maybe, this is it," thought Pete as he listened to
this chiseled soldier lay out his web. They promised
excitement, travel…and the GI Bill. They promised
a career and a future. Pete was drawn in enough to
schedule a visit to the local recruiting office. Though

the young recruiter pressed Pete to sign up that day, he chose to take the paperwork with him. He never leaped into anything…only after careful consideration. As he left the recruiting office that day, a blue and silver brochure rack caught his eye. He picked up a booklet on the Air Force Academy.

By the time the bus had arrived at his stop, Pete had digested the information and had made up his mind. Without a doubt, he knew the Air Force Academy was where he must be…and his ticket out of town. "Education first," as his priest had always told him. "They can never take that away from you."

Selection to attend any of the military academies centered around three evaluated areas of leadership, academics and athletics. The athletic element was straightforward. Did you or didn't you? Were you a participant or not? Team sports ranked higher than the individual sports, for they displayed qualities of teamwork and building relationships. Athletic abilities can be demonstrated through sport participation and achievements and validated through strength and agility testing. Likewise, the academic component was evidenced through class standing and SAT scores. Leadership was more subjective. Did the applicant hold class, team or club officer positions? Was Scouting in the resume? Eagle Scouts ranked especially high. An academy is basically a leadership school with the ability to hand-pick those with the highest proven leadership potential. Pete scored high in all areas and was selected by his Congressman to attend.

Pete had never been 'out West', except in his vivid imagination, and envisioned weathered cowboys with hand-rolled cigarettes dangling from their lips. He envisioned lots of open space, endless prairies and cactus, and saloons with wooden swinging doors. How surprised he was as the airplane let down through the high overcast into Colorado Springs when he saw the majestic Rockies for the first time, rugged yet so lush and green. There were even some small patches of snow left atop Pike's Peak. "Today," thought Pete, "is truly the first day of the rest of my life. This will be my home from where I will depart...but will always return. This is my touchstone...my life. Tomorrow will start a new life for me...as a cadet, a scholar, a pilot, an officer in the US Air Force." Pete thought how sappy that all sounded, but he was determined to break away from his boyish past and become a man.

3

Dave Edwards came to Colorado as a wide-eyed 18-year-old from a wide spot along a Montana state highway. He had ventured away from the natural beauty of those beautiful yet weathered Bitterroot Mountains only twice...once to sell some horses up near Calgary and again to fish the mouth of the Columbia with his Uncle Matthew. The sight of the Pacific always stuck in his mind. Like many before, he couldn't help but wonder what lay beyond that hazy horizon. Little could he have understood what fate held in store for him out there. But he seldom lost sight of his mountains and never got them out of his heart.

Like any other young man of the mountains, Dave challenged everything...especially himself. He was his own worst critic. He could accept flaws in others, but never in himself. No one was harsher on Dave than Dave...but in the most constructive of ways. And quite frankly, his own opinion of himself, though always positive, was the only opinion that really ever counted with him. He was his own best friend...and much of his time was spend outdoors, by himself. Dave never thought of himself as a loner...just happy with whom he was, wherever he was. He never had much and needed less.

Driven as he was, Dave excelled at much...in about everything he tried. His preference was for individual sports where his success...or failure...was all on his own drive and ability. He wanted to challenge everything on his own terms. And when he failed, he wanted only himself to blame. Boxing became an early love and passion for Dave through the local Boys Club. Though smaller in stature, he trained hard and found boxing a means to grow in strength and to threaten those larger and older than he. Maybe it was a power thing; maybe it wasn't. You didn't mess around with Dave without the expectation that he would come after you with the vengeance of a Grizzly protecting her cubs...and he seldom lost. But he lost the passion for boxing when he dislocated the arm of a good friend in a sparing match. He only put on the gloves one more time after that. But by this time, Dave was strong and tough and never turned away from a challenge.

The mountains always called to Dave. He loved the solitude, the smell and the sounds. He loved the thrill of hearing a bull elk bugling on a crisp autumn morning. And although Dave wasn't much into the social side of life, he loved the mountain people.

There was an old cowboy who worked the ranch down the road from the Edwards place. Dave always liked Billy, and they fished together when they could both get some time away from the chores that accompany living rough. Billy was an individual like Dave...but more of a loner and burned out on passion and life in general. He was a good hand, and that's about all you could say about Billy. But he shared a bit of his hard-earned wisdom up on Flathead Lake one evening around the fire. "Dave, you can never climb the same mountain twice." Dave didn't understand what Billy meant, for he had topped every mountain in the county at least twice and probably many more. Dave loved to hunt and fish and just get away to the solitude of the mountains. This was his turf and his home.

Dave loved to play poker and knew when not to respond when a response was expected...and how that threw others off guard. But Billy was also wise and knew that the silence to his shared philosophy meant only that Dave really didn't get it. He didn't understand why one could never climb the same mountain twice. Billy continued, "You see, son, you change and the mountain changes. What was will never return exactly the same, and you are growing and changing and becoming a man. You'll be leaving here soon, and things are gonna change...forever. That's just the way it is." That was the last time they fished, and Dave never saw Billy again. But he would never forget the lesson learned across the camp fire under the Big Sky.

When Dave Edwards left Montana, he was like a rich fertile field, scraped and plowed...ready for whatever was to come. His mind was quick, but his hands were quicker. He had already challenged life and knew how it felt to win...and to lose. He had made friends and made lovers. He had sampled the finest of life as he knew it, but knew there was more. He had never flown in an airplane, but wanted to learn to fly. He had never been east of the Rockies but wanted to see the world and make it his. He was leaving a world without fences and entering one of sidewalks and parking lots, stop signs and one-way streets. Dave entered the next stage of his life by hopping an east-bound freight train into Billings and rode shotgun in a cattle truck heading south through Denver to Albuquerque. It was summer of his 18th year, and life was good.

They told Dave not to bring much when he came to the Air Force Academy, that the Air Force would supply him everything he needed. In fact, when he told that truck driver good-by at the truck stop in Colorado Springs, he had half of everything he still owned in his old canvas backpack. Dave wasn't much for stuff. Those things he held of value were in his mind and in his heart.

Dave had some time to kill and no immediate plans so he wandered into the vacant truck stop to check things out and grab some chow. It had been too long since breakfast, and he figured he could get a burger and perhaps some information about this place. He was always curious and never shy in asking questions. He'd rather deal from knowledge, for good or for bad, than grovel in the what-ifs.

He figured the girl behind the counter to be a bit older than he, but she was a typical mountain girl...too much sun, too little make-up and no clue to what color her hair used to be. She flashed him a familiar smile as if she already knew him and motioned for him to take a seat at her counter. She held up an empty coffee cup, and Dave nodded. She leaned over the counter in the provocative manner that only waitresses can seem to master and very slowly filled his cup, never taking her eyes away from Dave's. This was a new brand of poker for Dave who didn't know whether to fold or up the ante when she asked him, "You wanna cream, Sugar." Dave was enjoying the moment and the view too much to hasten an answer. His slow response and admiring and probing gaze both startled and flattered her. He was certainly something new in town.

She continued after a moment. "I'll bet you the cost of this coffee...and even a meal, that I know more about you than you do about me." Dave had no idea who this girl was or where she was coming from, but it was worth the bet just to keep the conversation going...and neither knew where it was really going. But he could hope. "You first," she said. "Tell me about me."

Dave scanned her slowly and deliberately from top to bottom...and back to the top, pausing somewhere in between. The heat building in his gut reminded him of other days and other encounters. She wore cut-off jean shorts and hiking boots. Not the hiking boots you see in the catalogue, but the scuffed ones that show the miles. One boot lace was broken and retied. Her blouse was probably starched and white at the beginning of her shift, but not now. Her only jewelry was a turquoise cross dangling at precisely the right spot and a leather string of colored beads on her wrist. "Okay, I'm ready," said Dave.

"You're 19. Your name is Dawn, and you don't have a boyfriend."

"I'm almost 20, and I do have a boyfriend...sort of. But how did you know my name?"

"The tip jars say Dawn and Mariam...and you don't look like a Mariam."

"Okay, you're good. But what else?"

"You were raised here in Colorado and used to love to ski. But since your skiing accident 3 or 4 years ago, you had to quit. Now the only time you get to spend in the mountains is back-packing...which you do every week-end you can get off. You are torn between going into the mountains and being in church on Sundays. And lately, the mountains have been winning. You justify it in your mind because you figure you are closer to God when you walk the mountains." Dave paused a moment to check Dawn's reaction and continued. "Your worst habit is that you can't quit smoking...even though you really want to. And you wish you had more money to spend on getting your nails done every week." And then another pause...just for effect. "And one thing I really like about you...you don't like to ride on a motorcycle; you like to drive it yourself. I'll bet it's a trail bike. Right?"

"Boy, you are scaring me. How do you know all of this?"

Dave took a slow swig on his coffee to enjoy this moment of victory. "Well, your dress and complexion tell me you are a mountain girl. The V-shaped scar on your knee tells me you had a knee operation, probably due from skiing, and they switched over to arthroscopic surgery several years back leaving the three little holes instead of the scar like yours. Your shorts and boots show signs of lots of miles in the mountains. And there is pine tar on your boots. Your raspy voice is from your smoking, and the starched white blouse you probably put on this morning tells me you take pride in your looks. And that led me to guess about the nails."

"You don't know just how close you are. But tell me about my trail bike. Did you see it parked outback?"

"No, you have a black smudge on top of your left boot from the gear shifter. I'm guessing it's a trail bike 'cause I think you really like these mountains, like me, and wish you were up there."

"I do wish I could spend more time up in the trees, but I need to work some pretty long hours here. And I never seem to have enough money for nice things."

"Oh, you look great. Things will get better. You just have to be ready when the opportunity comes along."

"I know what you mean…and that's why I know so much about you." Dave's curiosity was racing. "You are 18, just graduated from high school really high in your class, maybe number one. Like me, you love the mountains, but you come from up north…maybe the Dakotas or Idaho…and lived on a ranch or a farm. But you are a dreamer and are ready to grab all of life you can. You are ready to leave the old life behind and go for it. You love sports and play hard. You could make it either on your physical talents or on your IQ, but you figure that using your brain rather than your back will get you further and faster. And I won't offer you a cigarette 'cause you don't smoke. I'm surprised you even drink coffee. And I don't have a clue what your name is. So how am I doing otherwise?"

Dave smiled and relaxed a bit. "My name is Dave Edwards, and you are very close. This may be a draw. But I grew up on a ranch in Montana. So how did you figure me out?"

"Well, I guessed you were from up north because I saw you climb out of that south-bound cattle truck…and the wear on the inside of the legs of your jeans tells me you spend a lot of time on a horse. And those worn-out old boots tell me you're no drugstore cowboy."

"Bingo. But how did you guess the rest about the sports and being a dreamer and high school?"

"Those of us here in Colorado Springs, especially the young ladies, know when the new class comes to the Academy each June, right about now. It's always in the Rocky Mountain Gazette. And we see you guys hit town all at once. Several thousand handsome, athletic, intelligent, competitive guys, who in about four years will be graduating…with a job and a career…and just maybe looking for a wife."

"Is that what you're doing, looking for a husband?"

"You got a problem with that? I never intended to go through life alone. Do you? Why fish in a shallow stream when the pickings are so good out there at the Academy? That's why I moved over here from the Gunnison Valley. I've dated a few of the cadets and kinda have my eye on one in particular. I'd tell you his name, but that might be dangerous information for you to have. He's a junior, I think, a Second Classman. Well, he'll be a Firstie when classes start again in the fall."

"I guess I never thought of it that way...girls and cadets, I mean. I guess I never thought of it at all. Too many other things going on in my life, you know. Go on."

"You had to rank high in your school class and excel in sports to even be invited to come. You guys are hand-picked, the cream of the crop...and every eligible girl from Idaho to New Mexico, Utah to Missouri, knows it. Cadets are fun to date, but they usually can only get out on the week-end. They're usually horny as hell, and do they love to spend their money and party! Come Sunday night, I'm usually ready for him to go back out to Cloudland and give me some rest."

"Wow, I never thought about any of this. I just came here to get an education and my wings and see the world...and to get out of Montana. Tell me more."

"Well, you won't get out much your first year. The girls who date Doolies or Freshmen usually go out there. It's tough if you don't have a car...and by the way, I do. There are things to do, but the Doolies have few chances to get off the Academy. And they have to wear their uniforms just about everywhere...so it's kinda weird. But it's really okay because everyone does it. But if a local dates a cadet, she has pretty much nixed her chances to date any of the local guys...except the Army guys out at Fort Carson...and that's not all that cool."

"Sounds like my Academy education just got started a day early. So why don't you come show me the town? Sounds like it's my last night of freedom for a while."

"Thanks, but I'd better pass. Like I told you, I'm already dating a cadet, and Charlie wouldn't like it." She paused a moment and then asked Dave to see his billfold, which he laid on the counter. Dawn took a page from her order pad, blotted her baby pink lipstick on it, and carefully wrote her name and phone number on it. She folded it and tucked it safely in Dave's wallet. "Just in case you need to talk sometimes. Now how about something to eat?"

Dave hardly remembered eating the hamburger. He was intrigued and somewhat mystified by his new friend. As he finished, Dawn came from behind the counter, took Dave's hand as if to shake it, but she placed it on her hip. She then gave him a gentle kiss on the cheek. "Good luck tomorrow. I hear it's pretty strange out there for you new guys. And don't forget," as she patted on the billfold in the hip pocket of his jeans. She suggested he go over to the YMCA near the bus station to clean up a bit, to shed that stench of the cattle truck before starting out to the Academy the next day.

Dave was confused by the mixed signals coming from Dawn. He had never encountered a woman quite like this. She had sucked the macho right out of him. He revisited his encountered with her as he walked the three blocks to the Y and pondered. There was chemistry between them, but then there's a chemistry between matches and gun powder. At least he got a good meal, made a new friend, and most of all, picked up a lot of good insight that would help him get through the next phase of his life. And he would be watching for this guy named Charlie.

* * *

Dave was pumped that Monday morning. He had
worked out and even jogged north along Nevada
Avenue. He loved the crisp, thin mountain air and the
burn it left in his lungs. He had toyed with the idea of
running all the way out to the Academy, but the lady
at the Y told him it was about 20 miles out there. And,
she reminded him, Colorado Springs was over 5000
feet in altitude and the Academy is over 7000 feet. He
cleaned up, threw his meager belongings in the canvas
backpack, and headed for the bus station. He figured
this to be a long and stressful day…and he wasn't
wrong.

As the bus entered the South Gate of the Air Force
Academy, Dave was expecting to see cadets marching,
lots of olive drab stuff, jeeps and airplanes. What
he saw was just more green mountains, a few low
aluminum buildings and a lonely railroad track
carrying an empty coal train back north toward his
home in Montana. He was glad not to be on that train.
That life was behind him.

A lonely Cessna was lifting off from a runway just to the north. And a tow plane was about to take off with a slender yellow glider in tow. But this was still not the Academy he had seen in the pictures. Where were the rectangular buildings of aluminum and glass? Where was the Parade Ground? Where was the silver Cadet Chapel with the 17 spires? Where were all the Corvettes he heard the seniors drove?

The bus turned west just past a football stadium and started a long climb up towards the mountains. The altitude even took its toll on the old bus. Soon the Cadet Area came into view. Everything was aluminum and glass…and very green…nestled out in the middle of lots of pine trees and foot hills. Immediately behind these four or five very large silver buildings lay the Front Range of the Rockies, rising another 2000 feet or so. My God! It looked like a modern Noah's Ark sitting atop Mt. Ararat. It wasn't Dave's Bitterroots, but it certainly impressed this young mountain man.

The bus stopped at the base of a large marble ramp that passed through a portal in a long marble wall that was probably three stories tall. Above the portal were chiseled the words, "Bring Me Men". From above, Dave could hear voices…no, more than just voices. There was shouting…lots of people shouting. And the response to the shouting seemed to be only "Yes, sir" and "No, sir". Before Dave could entertain second thoughts about what he was getting into, the bus driver closed the door and drove away.

A man dressed sharply in fatigues and with stripes on his sleeve greeted Dave in a friendly yet formal manner and asked Dave to follow him to in-processing. Up three flights of marble stairs in a series of glass meeting rooms, there was table after table...all in a row. Dave was coached in filling out a variety of forms. He wasn't sure of what all he had signed up for, but the lady at the last table smiled at Dave, pointed toward the door, and wished Dave good luck. She seemed to enjoy her work in a sadistic way.

Beyond that door, Dave found the source of all the shouting. Three upperclassmen dressed in starched fatigue uniforms pounced upon him like cats on a three-legged rat. The shouting began. "Stand at attention. Suck in that gut. Eyes straight ahead. What's the matter with you? Get those heels together, dirt bag. Where are you from, plow boy?" Before he could answer, another upperclassman demanded Dave drop for 20 push-ups. A piece of cake, thought Dave, and started down. The upperclassman went down, too, and challenged Dave as to who could finish first. Dave thought he was doing well until he noticed the upperclassman was only using one hand. That impressed Dave.

The next two hours went along about that same way with lots of "personal attention" from the upperclassmen and lots of shouting. In that short span of time, Dave learned to march in a straight line and turn square corners. He learned that the only answers he could utter were "Yes, sir," "No, sir," "No excuse, sir" and "Sir, I do not know." He learned to walk only along the edges of open areas and hallways...and to always keep his eyes on the floor. They gave him a serial number and took away his name.

Dave was never much good at taking this kind of abuse, but his uncle had survived Marine boot camp and had given him some good points of advice. First of all, the upperclassman yelling in his face was no better than Dave and had himself gone through this same treatment just a year or two before. If he could do it, then so could Dave. The only difference between Dave and his upperclassmen was a biological accident. Secondly, consider it as an initiation. You cannot get from here to there, from entry to graduation and flight school, without going through it. Everybody does it, and so could Dave. And finally, nothing lasts forever. Keep a sense of humor and stay the course. It will be worth it. That message would ring continually in his ears for the next year…even later when he himself was an upperclassman.

One upperclassman was placed in charge of ten of the new cadets and marched them down one floor to the barber shop. There were piles of hair everywhere. When it was Dave's turn in the chair, the barber smiled callously and asked Dave how he wanted his hair cut. Before he could answer, the barber had run the shears the full length of his scalp, cutting it down to stubble. Dave mused that lots of people ask questions here but never wait for an answer. He never realized how ugly a shaved head was…but then everybody had one.

From there, he marched with his nine classmates down to supply. Here they were issued everything they needed…just as he had heard. They even issued boxer shorts. Dave had never worn boxer shorts in his life…but he knew better than to make an issue of it. With three heavy laundry bags filled with boots and uniforms and shoe polish and boxer shorts and such, he was marched up to the 6th floor to his new room. He thought he would have no trouble with the altitude, but by the time he reached his room, he was seeing black spots and wanted to vomit. Dave, now Cadet Fourth Class Edwards, 2245K, was soaked with sweat and wanted to go to his knees. But his uncle's words toughened him up. If this guy yelling at him could do it, then so could he.

An upperclassman named Stebinski took over and marched Dave down the hallway to his room. "Git in this room, and put all this crap away. There's a Reg Book on your desk. Fold everything exactly as it's shown there. Exactly...and put it in the right drawer. Do you think you can do that, plow boy?"

"Yes, sir!" responded Cadet Fourth Class Edwards, standing at attention in the doorway of his assigned room.

"You got thirty minutes. Git to work."

The Reg Book showed exactly where everything went...which drawer...which shelf. Everything had to be folded to an exact size...and there was a ruler among the issued supplies to ensure it was done right. Even the damned boxer shorts had to be folded to an 8 by 8 square with the elastic at the top and the fly in the front...no wrinkles!

Dave had just finished emptying the last bag with everything put away...according to the Reg Book... when Stebinski returned. Stebinski looked like a linebacker for the Chicago Bears. He had no neck and

no hair. His starched khaki uniform looked perfect in
every respect. Dave thought that he must not ever sit
down, for there was not one wrinkle in his pants. And
his shirt looked as if it were painted on. If he were ever
in a bar fight, he knew he wanted Stebinski on his
side.

"Come to attention when I enter your room, you dumb
squat." Dave popped up to attention, heels together,
chest up, eyes straight ahead. "You finished?"

Dave replied, "Yes,sir!"

Stebinski pulled out the top drawer of the chest to
inspect Dave's work. "Re-fold these socks," grunted
Stebinski..."and these boxer shorts..." In an apparent
act of disgust, he pulled the drawer all the way out and
dumped all of its contents on the floor. Then he did
the same with the second and third drawers, throwing
them on Dave's bunk. He strutted over til he was
nose to nose with Dave. "You're in the Air Force now,
boy. You'd better learn to do it right the first time...
according to the Reg Book. Can't you read? Just how
stupid are you? How did you ever git in this place? Are
you the best that the Great American Public could
send us? If so, the whole future of the Air Force and
this country is in the toilet." Every instinct Dave had
was to take a swing at Stebinski...but was countered
by two simple thoughts. Stebinski could probably
bench press him with one arm...and his uncle's words.
Nothing lasts forever. Keep a sense of humor and stay
the course. It will be worth it.

Dave had just finished re-folding everything and
replacing the drawers when Stebinski re-entered

the room, smashing his fist against the door, with all the grace of a Corsair hitting the carrier deck and snagging the last cable. Dave spun around and stood at attention, finding him again standing nose to nose with Stebinski. "Well, sweetness, you got a roomie," he whispered. "Git your butt in here, loser!" he yelled back toward the door.

"There's only three things you two queens gotta remember," Stebinski grunted as he strutted back and forth between the two new cadets standing rigidly at attention. "I decide whether, when and if you eat, sleep, shit, shine, shower and shave...whether you live or die. You're mine. I own you. It's that simple. Secondly, I don't know how you two got in here, but I will do all I can do to wash you out...make you pack up your shit and go home to your mamas. You got it? I said, you got it!?"

"Yessir!" responded the two in unison.

To impress his point, Stebinski got nose to nose with each of the two new cadets, then without another word, pressed his index finger into Dave's chin, creating another wrinkle in the back of his taut neck. He wheeled about, stormed out of the room and slammed the door.

Dave and his new roommate continued to stand at rigid attention for ten seconds that felt more like ten minutes. Dave finally offered, "Why are we standing at attention? The gorilla has left the zoo."

He turned to his roommate and offered his hand. "Dave Edwards...more recently known as 2245K...

proud owner of this government issued M-1 rifle number 91336."

"Pete Benedetto...and I haven't been here long enough to even learn my serial number. And I didn't even know there was a number on a gun."

"Well, the first thing you gotta learn is that there's a difference between a rifle and a gun. It cost me fifty push-ups to learn this. "This is my rifle, and this is my gun. One's made for killing; the other's for fun."

"Got it. Thanks. Seems like there is going to be a lot for me to learn. So where do you call home, Dave?"

"Montana," replied Dave. "And you?"

"Well, I came here from Philly...and glad to be out of there. So I guess I'm still looking for a place to call home. This may be it for the next four years...unless Stebinski has his way."

"Hell, don't worry about him. He's just playing the role. A couple of years ago, he was standing right here just like you and me...and some upperclassman was screaming at him. He survived. He made it. And if he can, so can you. And so will I."

* * *

5

Regardless of one's pedigree, four years at any military academy is a tough road to travel. It's designed and redesigned to be that way. Only the best are invited to enter, and maybe half will still be there on graduation day four years later. Every aspect of a cadet's life and performance is designed to be challenged...and measured. There is no level entitled "good enough." Just when one reaches that level of being good enough to be continued...or promoted...or graduate, someone raises the bar. No cadet ever left the Air Force Academy knowing he was the best or perfect. The constant pressure and drive for the elusive target of perfection takes its toll, but for most, the journey is of a value only fully understood by those who have completed the trip.

Dave and Pete were both good cadet material. They entered well prepared mentally, physically, spiritually and academically...but not financially. Both were hungry for adventure, for growth, for a career...and for a way out of their past lives and into an exciting and challenging future. They shared a belief that this was either their ticket out or their ticket in...or both. It didn't matter to either. They were running neither from something nor to something...but they were running. They were committed to the journey without knowing the true destination. And that's okay.

Likewise, neither had a Plan B, an alternative. They were living fast and flying low...and neither owned a parachute. This was it for them. All the chips were pushed to the line. Except for a sixteen-dollar pair of worn-out Converse All-Stars, Pete had thrown away the South Philly clothes he wore to the Academy. And all that was left in Dave's old canvas backpack was a half roll of TP and his old Nocona rough-out cowboy boots that still smelled of horse sweat.

It was this focus and this determination that supported the duo through their first summer at the Air Force Academy. If the demons of Hell could be bottled, they would fizz in comparison to the first two and a half months there in the shadows of the Front Range of the Rockies. Every minute of every day seemed to echo Stebinski's threat. Every upperclassman was Stebinski's first cousin, committed to finding every weakness and then using it in eliminating every one of their classmates. No individual cadet could stand up to the constant pressure and harassment...and many didn't. Like inmates in a prison camp, survival depended upon cooperation. Politics, incarceration and boot camp create strange bed fellows. Cooperate and graduate was the necessary combination. That was precisely the paradigm the upper class was trying to force upon the freshman class...but they had to learn the lesson by themselves...as a class. Running with the herd and as a herd was a concept little known or appreciated by such a gathering of these high achievers, but necessity is a proficient professor. Those horses who strayed from the herd were soon devoured by the hyenas.

That first summer was extremely physical. Cadets marched or double-timed everywhere they went outside. Every day started with a run to The Rock and back. Cathedral Rock was a pair of natural sandstone towers two miles down a dusty road. The run was always in combat gear and carrying an M-1 rifle... usually above your head. The Doolies ran in formation, three columns of a dozen or so cadets each, with the upperclassmen scattered around the outside of the formation, prodding and engaging the Doolies with their insults and harassment. The challenge for the Doolies was to set a pace that the weakest cadet that day could handle. The pressure from the upperclassmen, of course, was to pick up the pace to cause one to drop out. When one Doolie weakened, others would encourage him and even carry his M-1 if necessary. No one was left behind. No horse was allowed to fall from the herd...even at 7000 feet above sea level.

Every day also included formal organized physical activities such as group calisthenics, where cadets learned to appreciate the joy of the 8-Count Push Up and the Squat Thrust. There were also formal physical training classes where Dave learned a life's lesson in what was called boxing class. It was more like street fighting but was called boxing to give it some legitimacy and to keep it out of sight of parents and

congressional oversight committees. Dave was already
an experienced boxer but had lost his taste for it.
During one of the practice sparing matches with a
classmate, Dave was primarily defensive, successfully
defending himself against his larger opponent, but
obviously non-aggressive in counter-punching. One
of the upperclassmen trainers stopped the match
and challenged Dave to be more aggressive. When
his prodding went obviously without result, the
upperclassman climbed into the ring and took the
gloves from Dave's opponent. Dave didn't like the
looks of this.

Once he had tightened the laces of his boxing gloves,
the upperclassman walked just into Dave's range and
shoved him backwards with both gloves. "What's it
gonna take to make you fight, pussy boy?" Again he
shoved Dave back into the ropes and took the boxing
position with feet shoulder width and gloves up to
protect the chin. The upperclassman fired a left jab
at Dave's face, which Dave's easily blocked with his
right glove. Then came a one-two combo. Again Dave
blocked the left jab, but the right cross got through
high on Dave's left cheek bone. Dave felt that one
and understood that this guy was out to make a point.
Dave really did not want to fight him, nor did he want
to stand out in the crowd...either as a pussy, as the
upperclassman continued to call him, or as one to take
out an upperclassman, which he felt he could probably
do. That right cross still stung as another one-two came
his way...and then another. Although he knew better,
Dave had had enough and tried to buy some time by

circling to his left and out of the corner of the ring. "Come on, pussy boy. Don't you want to take a swing at me? Come on and show your pussy classmates what a stud you are." And then he spit at Dave.

Dave uncoiled a lightning one-two-three at his opponent. The left jab drove both of the defender's gloves back into his own face, distracting him long enough to allow the right cross to land full force on his left temple. Both hands came down just as Dave fired his left hook up to the chin. The impact spun his opponent around as his unconscious body fell between the top and middle ropes and out of the ring. Dave had but one thought, "Oh shit, what have I done?"

He stood there for a moment that seemed like an hour, unlaced his gloves and threw them on the mat. His classmates cheered him, the worst thing, he thought, that they could do…both to Dave and to themselves. He tried to hide in the crowd and covered his head with a towel as he slumped down in the bleachers that surrounded the ring. But his classmates continued to cheer him. He knew he was in trouble…a marked man. You don't take out an upperclassman without some form of retaliation…and it didn't take long.

From beneath his towel, Dave saw a pair of black athletic shoes, the kind that only the upper class were issued. "Hey!" Dave pulled the towel from over his head to around his neck. Standing before him was a cross between Charles Atlas and Tarzan. This guy made Stebinski look like a Girl Scout. Dave popped to attention. "You've got a pretty good combination out there. Want to improve it?" he asked in a low, engaging voice.

Dave's ego and his military training gave him only one alternative as an answer. "Yessir," he belted.

"Oh, knock off the military crap. This is just you and me...two guys trying to be better boxers. Come on. I want to show you something." He tossed Dave his gloves and proceeded to lace up his own.

Dave looked over at Pete, who just shrugged his shoulders. He was no help. Dave really had no choice, but he did notice a predominance of upperclassmen hanging around. As Dave climbed into the ring still lacing his gloves, his challenger grabbed the top rope with both hands and bounded over it. This guy was about four inches taller than Dave and well developed...square-jawed with a flat nose. Dave was up to about any physical situation, but he just couldn't read what was going on here.

"Let's look at your one-two-three combination." Dave shadow-boxed through a couple of repetitions: left jab, right cross, left hook...left jab, right cross, left hook. "Your chance of connecting that initial left jab is slim, you know...unless you've already wounded him." His eyes twinkled. "It's only an attention-getter...a distraction. What you're really after is for it to pull his left hand forward in defense to allow that right cross to get inside." Dave grunted his agreement as the upperclassman went through the motions on him at half-speed.

"But now what I want you to do is to use both the left jab <u>and</u> the right cross as the distraction combination. Your opponent will be looking for that right cross… and you're going to give it to him…sort of…but not in the way he's expecting it. Instead of firing your right at his head, hit his gloves, both of them, in just a grazing shot. This will leave you in a position crouched down and to your left with your right up and protecting the right side of your head. But look at your position. It's perfect. You're protected. You're crouched down to your left, and you are ready to use your entire body, legs and arms to uncoil your left hook with every muscle in your body. It's especially effective against someone like me who's taller. Let me show you the motions."

Dave knew exactly what the upperclassman was talking about and mimicked his shadow-boxing motions. Dave was beginning to believe that this upperclassman was actually trying to help him polish up his combination. "Let's go a couple of rounds so you can try this."

The upperclassman told the time-keeper to ring the bell for two one-minute rounds, and at the sound of the bell the two cadets met at the center of the ring and bumped gloves. A bit of circling and jabbing led to Dave's first combination. None of the shots connected. The upperclassman fired a couple of jabs at Dave with moderate force…enough to get Dave punching a bit harder. In the first round, not much damage was done by either fighter. After all, it was only a sparring match. But in the second round, the force of both fighters increased, as did the speed. Dave was enjoying the contest and landed a couple, just as did his opponent. Yet he was glad when the bell ended the second round. He was ready to move on. He well understood the finesse of the one-two-three combination and readily absorbed the experience of what the upperclassman was trying to show him. Nevertheless, he really was not comfortable with what was going on.

"Good job, kid. I think you got the idea. Want to go another round…full speed? You can try out what you just learned." Dave was feeling pretty cocky now. He had held his own in the ring and felt he had impressed this guy with his abilities and style. Maybe he had seen this situation all wrong. He grunted his agreement and wiped off his face and gloves with a towel. Pete just groaned.

At the bell, both cadets met at the center of the ring, circled and fired a couple of jabs. Dave could feel from the force of the jabs that this was a strong opponent. But he had been here before and landed a few of his own. The spectators around the ropes were into it. They were watching two good fighters going after it… one an upstart, snotty-nosed Doolie and the other representing the entire upper class and the tradition of the rank structure. The fight was on. Dave got inside on the taller upperclassman and tagged him with a flurry of strong body blows until the upperclassman clinched him. Dave pushed him away and came back with his combination. He was going to put this guy away with what he had just learned. His left jab slipped between his opponent's forearms and landed squarely into his chest. He fired his right cross intending to graze his opponent's gloves to set up his killer left hook. But the upperclassman pulled back his gloves just in time to make Dave's right get nothing but air. The missed shot left Dave with his right arm fully extended and his head down and totally exposed. The upperclassman followed across and down with a left cross that caught Dave just in front of the right cheek. Dave felt his knees go limp as his body fell face first into the canvas.

* * *

Dave had no idea how long he'd been out when he started to regain consciousness. He just knew there were bright lights shining in his face and a couple of people bending over him. He was flat on his back in the center of the ring with a trainer on one side and Pete on the other. The room was clear of spectators now. They had come to see the show and got it. "How you doing, buddy?" Pete asked. Dave only moaned as he fought to clear his head.

"Who the hell was that guy?"

"Well, his friends call him Hoss," offered the trainer. "One hell of a fighter. Used to play football until he got crossed with the coach. Hoss told him to shove it and walked away. Strong as a bull...but a hell of a guy. He can be your best friend or your worst enemy. But you always want him on your side if you're in a fight. You probably didn't hear him because you were lying face down on the mat, but when he realized you weren't getting up, I heard him mutter, 'You never teach anybody everything you know.' And he didn't. The danger of that combination he taught you is that if your opponent expects or if you miss the right cross, both of which happened in your case, you are really exposed. He set the trap, and you went for it. Of course, if you had pulled it off, I'd be talking to him lying here on this canvas instead of you, and every upperclassman here would be lined up to take you on. It's the Law of the Jungle. As much as this hurts, it's the only safe way out for you, kid. Just tuck your tail between your legs, take a shower, and get on to dinner. Son, you just got a cheap lesson."

* * *

6

The Doolie summer is a unique flavor of Hell. It's not unlike combat where only those who have lived it can understand it…or even talk to each other about it. It seems comical and deadly serious at the same time. It seems to have no real worth or connection to reality while it is still the most important experience one ever encounters. It's simultaneously Sparta and Disneyland. No cadet on his first summer leave back home has ever successfully described that first summer or even the first year to his curious high school buddies. It's a bizarre yet fantastic system that creates a different breed of cat and sets its players on a course forever divergent from the ordinary and mundane.

Regardless of Stebinski's best efforts, Pete and Dave were not only surviving that first summer…they were devouring it. They challenged everything and usually won. And when they didn't, they savored and shared the lessons learned. Dave's hair trigger was tempered by Pete's focus and doggedness. Pete's journey with no destination often led him to question whether this was all worth it. Dave was always able to get Pete back on track and boost him with his pep talk about flying and challenging the world...and his uncle's words about how if the upperclassmen could do it, so could he. The system had put these two together, and it was a match made in Doolie heaven.

The greatest challenge came at the dinner table. The First Classmen, the seniors, sat at one end of each ten-man table; the Fourth Classmen, the Doolies, at the other. Other upperclassmen filled in the balance. Doolies sat at attention on the front six inches of their chairs with their chins tucked in and their eyes on their plates. They were not allowed to speak unless told to do so. The food was brought to the table and was received, announced and passed down the table by the Doolies. The First Classmen served themselves first, and if there was anything left by the time the dishes worked their way back down the table to the Doolies, they were allowed to help themselves. They ate only after each of their classmates had been served.

Doolies ate "square meals," meaning that the fork came straight up from the plate until at mouth level and then horizontally to the mouth. The bite size allowed was only what one could swallow after only three bites. With one's eyes down on the plate, it was impossible to see dripping or falling food, so Doolies' shirts often carried the remnants and stains of the meal.

Around the table, the harassment, although referred to as "training", was intense. The opportunity for a Doolie to get even a reasonable amount of food digested was marginal. Doolies were responsible

for learning, memorizing and reciting before
their table mates all sorts of information, such as
famous quotations, military history and facts, chains
of command, current news issues, and even the
opponent's strengths and strategies for the upcoming
Saturday's football game. Nothing was off-limits. Each
carried a small book entitled <u>Contrails</u>, about the size
of the New Testament and chocked full of history,
decorum, trivia, famous quotations and information
about the Air Force and the Academy. Every free
moment of the Doolie's day was spent studying and
memorizing in preparation for this table ritual.
And this was in addition to the rigorous academic
requirements.

The four keys to surviving the meal were good
peripheral vision to check the food levels on the
table [God help you if you ever let some food
item run out without reordering], eating quickly
without spilling something down your tie or shirt,
knowing your "Fourth Class knowledge" with enough
extraneous data to BS yourself through, and not doing
something stupid so as to draw the attention of the
upperclassmen. Although the upperclassmen seemed
to enjoy this system, the dinner table was not a friendly
place for a Doolie.

Dave was cursed with sitting at Stebinski's table,
and every meal was another chance for Stebinski to
pursue his promise. Stebinski was from somewhere in
the Appalachians and found Dave's Montana accent
especially annoying. In the third paragraph of The
American Fighting Man's Code of Conduct, a required
piece of Fourth Class memorized knowledge, it states

that if captured, "I will make every effort to escape and aid others to escape." But Dave's accent pronounced it as "excape", and this drove Stebinski into a rage. "Where the hell are you from?" demanded Stebinski. "Are you from some foreign country where they don't speak English? What's the matter with you? There's an s in that word. It's escape, escape, escape! You got it?"

"Yessir!"

"Why do I have to put up with these idiots? I have no clue how you got in here. Did you fall off some turnip truck at the South Gate? So where are you from?" He paused only to breathe. "I asked you a question. Are you going to answer it?"

Dave could feel the frustration building, and even worse, he knew that Stebinski was sensing it. "Sir, I come from Montana, sir!"

"You idiot! Only one 'sir' per statement! What's the matter with you? Pass in your plate, and sit there at attention. I want you to think about this Code of Conduct. It's important. And when you think you are ready to recite it properly...in proper English...stand up on your chair and recite in a strong voice that can be heard up there at Wing Staff. You got it?"

"Yessir!"

Dave knew this piece perfectly. He knew he could state it perfectly. He just clanked up under the pressure and frustration. But isn't this what it's all about? He wanted to get this over and perhaps get to eat something at this meal. He was ready.

"Cadet Stebinski, sir!"

"Think you can do it now, squat? Get on your chair!"

When Dave popped up to attention, the chair shot backwards and fell over. The sound of the heavy metal chair hitting the marble floor drew attention from tables around. Through his peripheral vision, Dave knew that Stebinski put his face down in his hands, either to cover his frustration or to cover his laughter. Dave didn't know which, but neither was a good thing. He felt like the total jerk, standing there at attention with everyone looking at him.

Stebinski very slowly rose from his chair at the head of the table and came around to where Dave stood. He got nose to nose with Dave, inches away from his face. Dave could smell the heat of his breath. It seemed like hours before Stebinski spoke. Frustration was rampant. Dave questioned in his heart why he really cared what Stebinski thought…but he did and wondered why. He was sharp and talented, but he knew he looked like a dolt in the eyes of the upperclassmen at the table. And he was too proud for that.

"Sonny boy," Stebinski said almost in a whisper. "You're embarrassing me, our squadron and your classmates. Everyone here in Mitchell Hall is looking at you and me. Even the officers up on the Staff Tower are looking. I'll tell you what we're going to do. I am going to pick up your chair since that seems a bit difficult for you today. You are going to stand on it and face the Staff Tower. Then you are going to recite it perfectly in a loud voice that will shake the windows in this place. You got it? By the way, your fly is unzipped."

Dave instinctively reached to zip his pants and found them already properly zipped. He looked at Stebinski, and the sadistic smile on his face made Dave know that he'd been had one more time. The anger and the frustration grew instantly, but he knew he had to work through it. He would have his chance. His focus at this moment needed to be on that chair and on his pronunciation. He was ready.

"Sir, The American Fighting Man's Code of Conduct. I am an American fighting man. I serve in the forces which guard my country and our way of life. I am prepared to give my life in their defense."

"I will never surrender of my own free will. If in command, I will never surrender my men while they still have the means to resist."

"If I am captured, I will continue to resist by all means available. I will make every effort to escape and aid others to escape. I will accept neither parole nor special favors from the enemy."

"If I become a prisoner of war, I will keep faith with my fellow prisoners. I will give no information nor take part in any action which might be harmful to my comrades. If I am senior, I will take command. If not, I will obey the lawful orders of those appointed over me and will back them up in every way."

"When questioned, should I become a prisoner of war, I am bound to give only name, rank, service number, and date of birth. I will evade answering further questions to the utmost of my ability. I will make no oral or written statements disloyal to my country and its allies or harmful to their cause."

As he started into the last paragraph, Dave knew he had conquered it and kicked in a few more decibels for emphasis.

"I will never forget that I am an American fighting man, responsible for my actions, and dedicated to the principles which made my country free. I will trust in my God and in the United States of America, sir."

Stebinski clapped slowly. "Sit down."

Dave stepped down from his chair and sat down. His plate was gone so he sat there with his chin tucked in and his eyes down. Dave was feeling a little bolder after his perfect recitation. "Cadet Stebinski, may I ask a question, sir?"

"No, you may not." Dave lowered his eyes back to the empty space where his plate used to be. As physical as it was to survive in this cadet training, Dave knew he had to get something to eat...either here or elsewhere. After a pause, Stebinski continued, 'So you're from Montana, from the mountains. I'll bet that you like buttermilk. You just love buttermilk, don't you, Mister Edwards?"

Even the thought of drinking buttermilk was vile to Dave. His dad used to drink it when Dave was young. He would stir a little pepper into it and pass the spoon around in front of the kids' noses. Yuk! Dave had never actually tasted buttermilk, but even the smell repulsed him. "No, sir!" Dave responded.

"I said that you loved buttermilk, didn't I? You love buttermilk, don't you?"

"No, sir!" Stebinski pounded his fist on the table and stood up, burning holes through Dave with his glare. "Yes, sir. I love buttermilk." Dave knew what was coming.

"Order yourself some buttermilk, Edwards." And Dave complied. He knew that if he even tried to drink it, he would surely vomit.

A quart of buttermilk finally arrived from the kitchen. The waiter set it on the edge of the table. Dave tried to ignore it, hoping Stebinski would forget and go off to afternoon class. He wasn't so lucky. "Pour yourself a glass," Stebinski ordered. Dave complied.

Dave knew that smell was first cousin to taste and figured that if he took a big breath and held it, he could get it down, neither tasting nor smelling it. He was not about to let Stebinski win this one. Dave picked up the glass, emptied it with one swallow, and banged the glass back down on the table. He choked back the urge to vomit.

"Wipe your mouth, son, and pour yourself another glass. You seemed to really enjoy it." Perhaps his bravado had backfired. Dave complied. Perhaps his dad's genes were present because somewhere back in Dave's mind, he actually and surprisingly kind of liked the taste…but he wasn't about to let it be known to Stebinski. He grimaced and shut his eyes. He thought about faking a gag but figured that to be too much. But after his second glass, he coughed and gagged a bit just for effect. Stebinski and several of the other First Classmen laughed and got up to leave the table.

Dave wasn't through with this game. It's tough to play to win with the upper class...but it be fun to try. They held most of the cards, but not all.

"Cadet Stebinski, sir. May I ask a question?"

"What do you want now, Edwards? I gotta go."

"Sir, may I have another glass?"

* * *

7

That first summer at the Air Force Academy had
basically been Boot Camp. Pete and Dave were beefed
up both physically and emotionally. They were ready
for the next step...the academic classroom. Now real
college was about to begin for their class...as real
as a college could be that existed solely to produce
professional military officers. It was still a trade school
with the singular goal of creating those who would
be comfortable living on the edge of society and
performing services for their country where many
would never understand nor appreciate their trade,
motivation and actions. The Air Force Academy was
lovingly known to the cadets as the Blue Zoo, and one
need not spend more than a day or two on this rock to
appreciate how unique, weird and effective this place
could be. For an outsider to explain the Blue Zoo and
its system would be like a man expounding on the
pain of child birth. One just had to experience it for
himself. The system would, of course, continue, but
now laid upon them was the academic challenge. The
cadet selection process had guaranteed that each cadet

in the class was capable of the heavy academic load, but with the additional pressure of the system, Pete and Dave knew they would be challenged...and that was a good thing.

Fairchild Hall was a monstrous shoebox of marble and aluminum, six stories tall and longer than a couple of football fields, home of countless non-descript classrooms, lecture halls and one hell of a library. Both the Commandant and the Dean officed there. Unlike Vandenburg Hall, the dorm, it was more aluminum than glass...boringly squared off and bleak. Cecil B. DeMille may have designed the uniforms, but he obviously wasn't asked about the architecture. The only adjective to adequately cover Fairchild Hall was functional. Not one item within its walls would detract from its main role...the academic excellence of its graduates. And what went on within those walls produced some of the finest scholars, engineers, pilots and leaders in the world.

The classes and the classrooms were small, with an excellent student-to-instructor ratio...about fifteen. All but a few of the instructors were Air Force officers with a Master's degree or higher. Many of the instructors were rated pilots, and many were graduates. But there were no cuts or walking in late, as each class was considered a military formation. Either be there on time, prepared and in proper uniform, or you paid the price...no exceptions. But then everyone was meeting those same requirements, so it made little difference.

Although the Air Force Academy is considered an engineering school by most standards, the list of core, or required, courses was significant and covered a wide range of topics. While heavy in the math, science and engineering, the core requirements also included English, Philosophy, Economics, Law, Political Science and Foreign Language. It was "equal opportunity" because regardless of how good a student any cadet was, there would be a class or two or more that would be out of his area and interest. There were a few 4.0 students, but very few.

Pete was a better student than Dave in general and in most disciplines. Both were good athletes and good students, but it always seemed to Dave that he had to work harder and longer to match Pete's grades. While both did well in the engineering courses, Pete seemed to glide through the soft and fuzzy courses such as Econ 101 and the Philosophy pipeline.

"How do you do it, Pete? I work my butt off to make a B and you're in bed before Taps. I don't know how you do it."

"Well, there's three things you gotta know...and they make this academic thing a whole lot easier. And I learned this when I was a Junior in high school...thanks to my priest back in Philly. First, he got me to take a speed-reading course. These 60-page reading assignments in History would be killers if I hadn't taken that course. It taught me how to read with discipline and control. It taught me what was important for the tests and what probably wasn't. I can read that paper-back novel while you're down taking your shower...and remember most of it."

"Then I took a memory course. One night on the
Tonight Show, Johnny Carson interviewed a guy
named Harry Lorraine, who was some kind of memory
expert. He and Jerry Lucas, the basketball player, wrote
a book on it. Before the show, Lorraine introduced
himself individually to everyone standing in line to go
into the show. Then when he came out on the stage,
he asked everybody to stand up and then sit down
when he called out their name. Dave, he got everybody
in the audience. He called out everybody's name. That
impressed me. I used to be really bad at remembering
names of people I met. I'm much better at it, but it
takes work."

"The trick is to make silly or exaggerated connections.
If a guy's name is John, I would picture him in my
mind carrying a toilet. See how stupid that is...but
it works. Let me give you an example. Your Cadet
Number is 2245. The way I remember that is to picture
you with a .22 pistol in one hand and a .45 in the other.
See how simple? You make a picture in your mind, and
revisit the picture when you need to use it."

"I'm sure those POWs in Viet Nam had a picture of the
tap code in their minds, as often as they used it and as
critical as it was. They didn't memorize that two taps
and then five taps was a "J". See, you look at the picture
in your mind. You got five rows and five columns...a
5 by 5 matrix. The top row is A through E and so on
until the matrix is filled. There is no "K", and numbers
have to be spelled out. In your brain, even words are
pictures. It's all about pictures. If you saw your name
written out...E...D...W...A...D...R...S, you would still
recognize it as Edwards. The tap code is the same way.

You form a picture in your mind and move down the columns and across the rows as the taps come. Your name would be one tap, then four, pause, one, one, pause, five, one, then one, five. D...A...V...E. Looking at a picture of it in your mine is so much easier than trying to put a tap combination with every letter... like the Morse Code. It's all about the brain and weird memory tricks."

"That's good stuff to know. I need to practice this."

"Well, the tap code isn't new. It was actually used in Ancient Greece and by the World War II prisoners. And it's easy to learn. I heard the POWs in Nam were fluent after only a couple of days. And you know it had to keep morale up...being able to talk to someone."

"Yeah, can you imagine what this place would be like if we couldn't talk to each other and to our classmates? It would be like a POW camp."

"I'm going to give you a totally useless piece of information that you will never use but will never forget. Mt. Fugi is 12,365 tall. There are 12 months in a year and 365 days in a year. And now you will never forget it.They might have that book over in the library. You need to give it a try. That's the way I remember the Atomic Weights on the Element Tables in Chemistry, and it helped me memorize and remember the Fourthclass knowledge stuff. I'm telling you, it works."

"Okay, okay, so what's the third thing?"

"Well, it builds on the first two, and it's how to spec a test. Nobody can remember every detail of every

subject we have to study. So what I do is try to figure
what will be asked on the test. I spec six questions and
write out an answer to each. Then like a politician in
a political debate, I use those answers and adapt them
to answer whatever question comes my way. Sure, I
have to wrap some BS around it, but it's usually good
enough to get a B…and sometimes an A."

"You need to be teaching a course on this."

"Well, it works for me. Have you ever heard the story
of the two guys out camping and a bear wanders into
their camp in the middle of the night. One guy is
running around wringing his hands wondering what
to do while the other guy is calmly tying his shoes. The
first guy says, "What are you doing? You can't outrun
that bear." The second guy says, "I don't have to. All I
gotta do is outrun you." It's the same way here. I don't
have to be at the top in grades, but I sure as hell don't
want to be at the bottom. Of course, I want to be high
enough four years from now when we graduate to get
my base of choice for flight school."

"Then you can mix them together. Let's say that you
figured that you needed to know all of the President's
Cabinet positions for a Poli Sci exam. If you knew
them, you could work them into an answer somewhere.
So you make a silly acronym or a rhyme of the first
letters of each Secretary…and you got it. Or take for
example the GUMP check we do during the final
turn in the flight traffic pattern…gas, undercarriage,
mixture, prop. That's a good example. And tell me
how many days there are in July. And if your birthday

isn't on the 31st, you'll most likely be doing the 'thirty days hath September' thing."

"Okay, okay, I'm convinced! It's like that song about the soldier who used a deck of cards for his prayer book. The Ace reminded him of Jesus. The three, the Trinity. And the Joker was Satan."

"I never heard of that song."

"Probably didn't get much play in Philly. You couldn't dance to it. Dick Clark probably never heard of it either. It's a country and western thing, city boy."

* * *

8

The first year at a military academy seems ten times longer than the following three. Every moment of every day is filled with challenge, stress and measurement. The harassment is unrelenting and focused uniquely on the individual's set of frailties. Pete and Dave found that their upperclassmen, especially Stebinski, were experts on finding an exposed wound and grinding salt into it with the heels of their boots. Doolies double-timed everywhere when outside. When inside any building, they were required to march at attention down the right side of the hall with their chins tucked in and their eyes on the floor... raising them only to greet passing upperclassmen with a booming "Good morning, sir!" Most cadets found that their peripheral vision became fine tuned...a nifty asset later on for these prospective pilots.

One night after the last note of Taps had finally faded away, Pete and Dave were lying in their bunks reflecting on the day's events. Their room was on the sixth floor, the top floor of Vandenberg Hall, and Dave liked to open the windows to the cool winter mountain air. It reminded him of better days in the Bitteroots with the full moon in the southeastern sky casting eerie shadows across the floor. Pete just liked breathing the Rocky Mountain air instead of the Philly stench.

"What do you think Stebinski is really like? Is he really such an asshole, or is this just part of the game?"

"Probably some of each, I figure. Remember, he's only two or three years older than we are. And in two or three years, there will be Doolies lying here in their bunks right here in this room wondering the same thing...if Edwards and Benedetto are really assholes. How about it? Are you an asshole?"

"No, but I'm working on it. Work in progress!"

"I figure if we can make it through this first year, we got it made. I guess my big concern right now is the academics. I know I can handle the rest of it."

"You wouldn't have gotten in here if you couldn't do the book stuff. It's not like Stebinski says. They're not here to wash you out. They're here to graduate you. They want us to succeed...and we will...one day at a time. We just don't do anything stupid...like break the Honor Code."

"Or punch out an upperclassman?"

"Yeah. That wasn't too smart. I'm still paying for that one."

"Yeah, but it opened some doors for you. When you look back on that in a year or two, I think you will find it was a good thing. At least people know who you are.

I'll bet you a Coke with ice that it turns out okay...a good thing."

"Maybe... Now shut up, and let's get some sleep. God knows we need it."

Pete wasn't ready to shut it off yet, but he, too, knew how it was important to get some rest when the time was available. He could probably sleep standing up if the opportunity arose...and he may have on several occasions. Like Dave, he loved the physical part of being a cadet. He loved the exercise and the athletics. He loved the feeling of growing stronger with every day. Already, he could tell that his chest and biceps were taking a more defined shape and that his neck was probably an inch or more larger. And this was a good thing.

Pete was different from Dave in that he framed every activity and challenge of the day into the big picture. Dave was more of a shoot-from-the-hip sort of guy... not a hair trigger...but quick to respond. Dave always said what was on his mind. Pete never said much... and he chose his words carefully. And often, he would put those words down on paper...and tonight was one of those inspired moments. He was glad Dave had fallen asleep already, for he didn't like exposing his vulnerable side to his bullet-proof roomie. He neither wanted to nor could explain his drive to write and the mystic mood that tended to overwhelm him. Perhaps his old man was right.

From his bunk, Pete could look directly across the darkened Terrazzo, the formation area, at the Cadet Chapel. Even at night there was some interior lighting in the Protestant Chapel that shown through the stained glass at the north end above the pulpit. The colored glass was so unique in the aluminum world of the Air Force Academy. It cast its lights eerily across the Cadet Area and the grassy area between the Chapel and Mitchell Hall, creating new shadows and shapes everywhere. After Taps when all is quiet and lights are dimmed, there is magic here, and Pete felt the spirits moving across the area. He recalled when he once hiked the road from Lexington to Concord early on a Sunday morning and could hear the anguish of the combat and even smell the stench of the black powder. Then, as now, he knew he wasn't alone. The spirits invited him into their revelry.

The breeze moved briskly down through Deadman's Canyon and whistled as it made its way through the maze of aluminum and glass buildings. In Pete's mind, there had always been something mystical about the Academy after Taps. Many thoughts and scenarios had run through his young mind over the past weeks, and he had awaited the right moment to get them down on paper. Tonight was the night. In his cool dark room, he began to write, holding his penlight in his teeth so as not to awaken Attila across the room.

With Chinook standing raw, mountains accent the pall
As yesterday's spirits abound.
On such cold winter's night, pray pity the plight
Of the mortal who enters their ground.

The ramp holds possessed by those who were blessed
With return with each Deadman's Chinook.
At night's mid comes perfect umbra of sun
And this flight with no element of luck.

Many have yearned yet so few have earned
The right to call Cloudland their home,
Shun glory and fame, succumb to the flame,
Unarmed, unafraid nor alone.

Many airmen were lost to that last river crossed
In their Phantom, Thud, chopper and Hun.
Each raced to beat hell and in victory each fell,
Live fast, love them all and die young.

In the cold crisp night air, senses standing aware,
Our spirits together rejoice.
The years can't erase the grin on each face.
The howling wind echoes each voice.

The flight is all present, the banter incessant.
Each boasting is followed by two.
No airman denies the right to tell lies,
For every war story is true.

This warriors' clan pleasures meeting again
For such spirited nocturnal mirth.
Each answers the draw of the Chinook's recall
To return to his heaven on Earth.

'Neath the wing of the Thud in a hot game of
stud
Crouched a six-pack of yesterday's free.
This iron Butterfly brought a new way to die
While hoping for Aces to be.

And the younger crowd so proudly avowed
The virtues of Falcon Sixteen.
Up cloud canyons led on this cold hot rod sled,
The bandit's nightmare machine.

A stranger to war, Mr. Lockheed's star,
The Foxtrot one-oh-four.
A lone pilot told how his soul had been sold
Through the rocket's bottom door.

Still the largest clique had gathered to kick
The tires of Phantom F-4.
Many had trusted; these many went busted,
But to her still allegiance each swore.

The queen of the fleet, always ready to meet
Each challenge that encountered the team.
Over-loaded and bent, and too often sent
To seek the impossible dream.

And in the Air Garden demanding a pardon
Were the original RTB's.
The talk was of Lowry and how they may now be
The basis of all histories.

And there were those whose final repose
Were simply marked with a plaque.
Their all they gave for an empty grave.
The Earth has called them back.

By the Fledglings were others awaiting their
brothers,
A place in the circle reserved.
Each rests now at peace waiting brother's release
From service so forlornly served.

Now they gather as one 'round the black granite stone
To pray for diversion from hell.
The howling winds dwindle; they make note of men
who will
Answer this year's passing bell.

One voice reads the list of anticipated guests
To join when the next Chinook blows.
For their families they pray, the wind dies away,
The compassionate ceremonies close.

When Orion stands tall and Deadman's blows raw
And the ramp reeks of glory and fame,
Trespass, if you will, but pray as winds still,
That they do not call out your name.

Yes, this is their ground and their spirits abound
At midnight when Chinook winds blow.
Please enter as friend, as comrade and kin,
And listen to tales long ago.

On the marble you find the footprints of time
Left by warriors gone before.
Acquire their tastes and inherit the space
That lies beyond June's open door.

These are your wingmen who are challenged to bring men
To fly and to fight and to win,
So wherever you go, always check six and know
In their circle you always are friend.

Pete loved being who he was, where he was, when he was.
He knew he was in the process, in the pipeline, a part of
the Long Blue Line…a line that included famed military
aviators such as Billy Mitchell and Jimmy Doolittle, Fast
Freddie Gregory and Wild Bill Sieg, the WGFP. He
silently acknowledged his pride for his position in that
line and would give his life for the honor.

* * *

9

A four-year stint in a military school sounds like a long time. Some weeks passed like months; others like minutes. Every moment of a cadet's day and life is spoken for in an Academy...either by the Dean and his academic hired guns, by the Commandant and his little Adolphs, or by the Director of Athletics and his muscle-bound protagonists. Each member of the triad owned a set number of those precious minutes and protected them like the family jewels. To a cadet, it soon seemed that he is only a number...not a person. You lived by the system, and you survived by the system. Either you did it according to the system, or you headed out the South Gate and joined the Great American Public. Although you were exposed to the finest of educations and became fit as a pentathlete, believing that this was real life was always a danger.

Four years of living on this rock could do weird and often wonderful things to any great American youth. It could transform a normal, high-performing teen-ager into a Rhodes scholar or an Academic All-American or just a super-Spartan prepared and ready to take on the world. Yet if one came to the Academy with a chink in his personality or a glitch in his logic, that same four years could create an abyss. Fortunately, most fit into the first category...but there were plenty of the others. The hazard was that hard work and perseverance were generally required and rewarded, and there were the unfortunate few whose perseverance and dedication never left the property nor the system. They just never seemed to get it that this was just a trade school...a damned good one...but still an artificial society designed to create good soldiers and airmen. The Academy was not an end of its own, but rather it was intended to be a cog in the process of protecting American freedom, security and dominance...and nobody did it better.

Academy life was one of high stress and extreme competition in every aspect...cadet vs. cadet, squadron vs. squadron, upper class vs. the Doolies, cadet vs. the academic system and the military system. Everything was tracked, graded and recorded. The good cadet learned to compete with everything and everybody while supporting the system and understanding that this was only a temporary and artificial environment. Real life started at the intersection of Interstate 25 and their fifth USAFA June. How well a cadet prepared for life-after-AFA determined the success of the previous four years.

And in that regard, Dave and Pete were significant parts of each other's education, maturity and growth. Although from differing backgrounds, they were so much alike in their shared motivations, spiritual beliefs, respect and love for each other, and trust and ambition for the future. They loved who they were and were becoming. In another life, they were probably brothers or lovers. Theirs was an unspoken pact to cover for each other, to always be there to "Check Six" for one another…wingmen for life.

Evidence of that occurred late in their Fourthclass year. As was custom, cadets shuffled their seating assignments in the dining hall on a regular basis. Pete and Dave escaped Stebinski's table, but neither his attention nor his wrath. The Firstclassman who headed their ten-man table was a lanky red-head from Macon, Georgia, named Bush who shared the general aversion for Stebinski, his mouth and his opinionated attitude. In his soft Southern accent, Bush addressed Pete. "Mr. Benedetto!" Pete swallowed what he figured would be his last bite for that meal. "Benedetto, there are no problems in life…only opportunities…and I am about to offer one to you. In the past nine months that you have been a cadet here at our beloved Academy, I have observed that one of my class mates has been rather focused on you and your roommate. And I must admit that you two have done a splendid job of surviving his continual assault. Our time here together, yours, mine and Cadet Stebinski's, is growing short what with our graduation's being only a month away. I think it's about time for a Suicide Mission. What do you think about that?"

Bush could tell by the blank look on Pete's face that he had no clue as to what was involved in a Suicide Mission. "All you have to do is to sneak over to Stebinski's table tonight at dinner. I suggest you crawl. Stebinski's table is two tables over. You need to brief your classmates that you are coming. They'll let you crawl in under the table. Then sneak up under the table and set fire to Stebinski's napkin. It's just that simple. What do you say?"

"Oh, shit!"

"That's 'Oh, shit, sir', Benedetto."

"Oh, shit, sir!"

"If you succeed, Benedetto, and I am betting on you, then you will get to sit at ease at my table for the rest of the year. No more square meals. No more sitting at attention for the next thirty days. Are you up to it?"

"Yes, sir! But under one condition."

"I don't normally barter with Doolies, Benedetto, but I'm growing soft in my old age. What's your deal?"

"If I succeed, and I plan to, then Cadet Edwards also gets to sit at ease."

"Okay, it's a deal...and that goes for any other Doolie that sits at my table. Now eat!"

"Yes, sir. I'll be ready. We'll be ready." The contract on Stebinski had been set. Pete used the tap code with his shoe against Dave's to send him the message. "Vengeance is mine, sayeth the Lord." Pete could sense Dave's smile without ever seeing it.

If he were to be able to pull this mission off successfully, Pete would need to be able to get to the floor and crawl unnoticed two tables down to Stebinski's. Any upperclassman who spotted him would know he was up to no good but would ignore him just to witness whatever was about to happen. It was the Law of the Jungle. When one is incarcerated in the bizarre academy venue for seven days a week, week after week, the standards of humor change. The only one whom he absolutely must avoid was Stebinski. He would clue in his classmates at that table so they would leave enough room for him to crawl in under their table. The challenge was how to escape after igniting Stebinski's napkin…but he had a plan even for that. If he were to fail, the thirty days left until Stebinski's graduation and departure would be an absolute hell. But success would secure him a place in the annals of "remember when" at all future gatherings of two or more cadets or grads. Yes, to Pete Benedetto, the risk was an opportunity and one he considered himself fortunate to have encountered.

* * *

Pete's plan was in place. He would have a butane lighter in each sock, as would Dave, just in case Pete's were discovered. All the players were briefed and ready. Win or lose, tonight would be the commencement of a new life for Pete Benedetto.

Getting to Mitchell Hall, the cadet dining hall, was an event in itself. Three times each day, each squadron of a hundred or so cadets would form up in their appointed area on the terrazzo. The upper class would inspect the shoes and uniforms of the underclass. An attendance report was given, the band would strike up the Washington Post March, and the parade to Mitch's began. Visitors to the Air Force Academy would clap their hands to see the cadets perform with their exacting precision. It got to be pretty mundane stuff for the cadets, but it had to be impressive to the spectators. Not unlike a stage production of Chorus Line, if one got far enough away, it looked like spit and polish, all in step and moving as one. What the distant observer failed to see was that each one of the cadets was an individual with individual concerns and issues. Pete was just one of those cadets. His heart was beating so rapidly, he wanted to scream to release the tension mixed with the fear and anticipation of what lay before him.

As each squadron arrived at the dining hall, the cadets were dismissed to find their way to their assigned tables. With their eyes on the floor, each Doolie would count rows of tables until they found their chair. In the chaos, Pete sneaked a peek down two tables where Stebinski was to sit. He was there already yelling at the three of Pete's classmates sitting at the other end of his table. Pete had briefed them on what to transpire and how they could help him on his Suicide Mission.

The cadet dining hall was the centroid of chaos and noise. Doolies were spouting off memorized knowledge at the demand of the upperclassmen. Other Doolies were announcing food as it arrived at the tables. The intense noise level and activity would provide Pete with some cover...but not enough. He had planned a diversion.

Pete was too nervous to eat. He thought he was going to puke. About halfway through the meal, he raised his eyes from his plate to ask Bush for permission to leave the table. The time had arrived. Bush was already looking at him, and when he saw Pete's eyes, he quietly nodded his head and flashed Pete a thumbs-up. Pete whispered to Dave, "Bingo!."

Dave stood to attention…his eyes on the floor. He marched smartly around the table and behind Bush's chair and toward Stebinski's table two tables down. As he passed behind Stebinski's chair, he intentionally tripped on the back leg of his chair and fell to the floor, drawing Stebinski's attention to his left and away from Pete, who was now moving toward the Doolie end of Stebinski's table. Stebinski's Doolies were in on the plan and had made room between their chairs for Pete to duck down and under the white table cloth. So far so good. He crawled the length of the table and pulled the butane lighter from his sock. All he had to do was wait for Stebinski to sit back down.

Stebinski was all over Dave, like flies on a dung heap. He was pulling out every pet phrase and insult and dumping them relentlessly on Dave, who was still sitting on the floor now feigning an injury to his arm. "Unless you're injured, plow boy, you'd better get on your feet when I'm talking to you. Git up, mister!"

Dave slowly responded, stalling for time, still nursing his arm, but finally got into some form of standing at attention. His Oscar performance had Pete, who was watching from only four feet away from under the table, wondering if perhaps Dave were really injured. Dave played his role to the hilt.

"Why do I have to put up with these idiots? You cannot be part of the cream of America's youth! This is a joke, right? You're a joke. Now git out of my sight." Stebinski threw his napkin on the table and started to leave the table. He told his roommate who sat next to him at the table, "I gotta go to the library to work on my Aero report."

Oh hearing this, Pete thought his whole plan was going to fall apart. He couldn't leave the table…not now that he had gotten this far.

"Just a minute," said Stebinski's roommate. "Sit down. There's something I need to talk to you about." Pete thought he'd been busted. He thought Stebinski's roomie had gotten wind of his plan and knew he was under the table. He was about to be exposed. The doors of hell were swinging open.

Stebinski sat back down, pulled his chair up to the table, and instinctively put his napkin in his lap. Pete's prayers were answered. "There is a God," he muttered to himself. He had only seconds to light that napkin and flee. One flip on the lighter did it, and he had backed out to the other end of the table just as Stebinski reacted to the flames in his lap.

Cursing, Stebinski pushed away from the table, stood up and beat at the flames scorching his crotch. He knew he'd been had and exploded with anger. This was the cue that all the Doolies in the squadron were awaiting. As if one, they all popped to attention, pushing back their chairs with such force that most chairs fell to the floor, causing the noise and distraction planned to allow Pete's escape. Then they began singing the 'Air Force Song', as custom and tradition required that every cadet, upperclass included, stand and sing all four verses and the chorus.

Everyone was standing and singing. "Off we go into the wild blue yonder…" Chairs and standing cadets blocked Stebinski's path and vision as he tried in vain to catch the assassin. "…climbing high into the sun." It was planned that one of the Doolies at the next table would slide one table over to fill Pete's chair, and Pete would then need to move only a short distance to be at a seat. "Here they come, zooming to meet our thunder." Pete's back was now turned to Stebinski. "At 'em, boys, give 'er the gun!" He wished he could see the results of his mission, but right now would not be a good time for Stebinski to see the Grand Canyon grin on Pete's face.

Pete looked over at Bush, and again they made eye contact. When it came to the part of the song that says, "We live in fame or go down in flame," Bush discretely pointed his finger at Pete and flipped him another thumbs-up.

Stebinski wasn't about to accept what was going on. Throughout the Air Force Song, he continued to swear and yell at the Doolies at his table. Then he recalled and reacted to Dave's earlier action of tripping on his chair, figuring rightly that it was a planned part of the hit. He went straight to Bush's table and got in Dave's face. Dave continued to sing.

"Plow boy, I know you had something to do with this." Dave continued to sing even louder. "I'll have your ass, boy! I'll have your ass! Do you know anything about this?"

"About what, sir?"

"You idiot! Do you know who set my napkin on fire?" he yelled in Dave's face.

"Napkin, sir?" Dave did not want to answer that question, for he was subject to the Honor Code and couldn't lie. But he was not about to tell the truth. He was in a real dilemma. He couldn't lie. He couldn't quibble. Yet he couldn't tell the truth. "On fire, sir?" He stalled for time trying to come up with a response. "I couldn't have set your napkin on fire, sir!"

"Dammit. I didn't say you did, you idiot. I asked if you knew who did it? Now are you going to answer me or not?"

"Stebi," yelled Bush, coming to Dave's rescue. "You can't ask him that question. You can't use the Honor Code to force him to reveal information."

"Like hell I can't," growled Stebinski.

"Stebi, I'm the squadron Honor Rep, and I'm telling you that you're asking an improper question. Don't cross me on this. I'm instructing Mr. Edwards not to answer that question."

The Honor Code at the Academy created some very odd bedfellows and even stranger situations. It overarched time and class, academics and military training. It was a cadet-created pledge that stated they would not lie, cheat or steal…or tolerate those among them who did. And tolerating was just as great of sin as lying, cheating or stealing. Cadets found guilty by their peers of committing any of the four were basically excommunicated and asked to leave. There was little gray area. Cadets wrote it and enforced it. Continual training was conducted by Honor Reps like Bush, and it was a constant within the cadet's life. Academic exams often were not monitored. Statements were not questioned. Truly, a man's word was his bond. Interesting situations came up, such as one cadet's concern whether he could tell a girl he loved her just to get in her pants. But one decision was basic: you could not use the Honor Code to force an incriminating answer. For Dave to answer this question truthfully, as he would be required to do under the Honor Code, he would be admitting guilt. Therefore, Stebinski could not force Dave to answer this "improper" question and should not have even asked it. And for Dave not to answer the question was just as incriminating. He was trapped on the bloody horns of dilemma.

Stebinski was breathing fire now. But Bush was not about to relent. "Let me see if I can help you, Mr. Edwards," stepping between Dave and Stebinski. "Would I be correct in assuming that every Doolie in the squadron knew of what was going to happen tonight?"

"Yes, sir. I think that would be a good assumption."

"And do you think that every upperclassman knew the details?"

"No, sir. Not every upperclassman."

"But some?"

"Yes, sir. Most likely."

"And do you expect that any cadet, Doolie or upperclassman, will ever reveal their knowledge of this incident to Cadet First Class Stebinski?"

"No, sir."

"And why not, Mr. Edwards?"

"It's the Law of the Jungle, sir."

"Cooperate and graduate, huh?"

Cadet Bush had led Dave to the right answers that had both covered for Pete and Dave and taught all within earshot of this conversation the importance of sticking together. One plus one can equal three for large values of one. Dave knew that it wasn't over with Stebinski, but he felt the protection of the crowd, like penguins huddling together when the birds of prey circle. And in less than a month, Stebinski would be in his Corvette heading out the South Gate for the last time. It had been a diary kind of night for Pete and Dave.

* * *

There were fifteen minutes between Tattoo and Taps, when lights had to be out. From the time cadets returned to their rooms after the evening meal until Tattoo, about three hours, the cadets' time belonged to the Dean. Everyone was restricted to academic duties. Sleeping was allowed…but no socializing. Soon after the bugle sounded Tattoo, Cadet Bush knocked on their door and entered.

"At ease, gentlemen. I think we need to talk about tonight's adventure. First of all, what did you learn?"

Pete started, "Sir, I learned that if Cadet Stebinski finds out who set fire to his napkin, I'm dead meat."

Dave added, "And he probably won't be too happy with you either, sir."

"Sir, why do you dislike him so much?" asked Pete.

Bush chuckled. "No, I don't dislike Stebi. Those of us who know him like him...and understand him. Let me tell you a little about Stebi. He loves the Academy probably more than any of us...and loves what it's done for him...and for each of us. He wants every person who graduates from this place to be as tough and as 'with it' as he thinks he is. That's why he is so tough on you Fourth Classmen. He wants you to have pride in the Academy and in yourselves and in your class. He wants you guys to fight back, to organize some resistance, to show some backbone...to set fire to some napkins. Just think about it. If a cadet spends four years here and never has to struggle or get mad or be afraid, then the Academy has failed its mission. This, gentlemen, is a trade school, where the system preps you for other days and other battles and other struggles. When you graduate, you will have placed in your hands and in your command a multi-million dollar airplane, or some mass weapons, or several hundred men to lead. Whatever you do, this is the place to develop your skills...not out there."

"Another thing. You put a feather in his hat when you struck at him. He takes pride that he pushed you to take a shot at him. He finally got you to strike back... not as an individual...but as a group. Tonight, Stebi is smiling...but you'll never see it. So don't worry about being discovered. He's not through with the yelling about this, but he doesn't want to know who did it. If he did, then he would have to punish you and that would be the end of it. He wants you and your classmates to have this secret and stick together to cover for you two guys. It's the Law of the Jungle. Do you understand?"

"Yes, sir."

"Yes, sir."

"So let me leave you with these two thoughts. "First, you did a good job in pulling this off. I'm proud of you. You carried off your part of the bargain, and I'll honor mine. Whenever you choose to sit at ease at my table, simply ask, and it will be granted. But remember that Stebi may wonder or suspect why. It's your call."

"But you haven't heard the last of Mr. Stebinski. We are all going to be out there in the real Air Force together doing our thing. He will haunt you…and me…until we each cross that last river. He will be your best friend or your worst nightmare. But he'll always be on your side of the table. Count on it! Good evening, gentlemen."

* * *

10

The remaining month until Bush and Stebinski and the rest of their class graduated and were commissioned as Second Lieutenants in the US Air Force passed quickly. The senior class had received their orders for their first real assignment and grew more FIGMO with each get-up. Most who were pilot qualified chose to attend flight school and would enter either A or B class soon after their June graduation at one of the Air Force Undergraduate Pilot Training bases spread across the southern tier of the US from Arizona to Georgia. The government had determined during the conduct of WWII that flying weather was better and more conducive to flight training in the south. All of the UPT bases had been around since those war days.

Like every other member of their Doolie class, Pete and Dave were happy to have survived their first year. Quite a few of their class had already washed out for one reason or another. That first year was treacherous, and the combination of the heavy college academic load and the Fourth Class system had taken its toll.

Some couldn't hack the stress and demands of the
military system. For some it was the physical aspect.
For others it was the academics. And a few went home
to take care of pregnancies. Some just simply changed
their minds on a military career…especially with the
looming clouds of war on the Korean penensula.
North Korea was showing more and more belligerence
toward the West, especially now that they have
exposed their nuclear potential and are known to be
developing a family of delivery systems. The realities of
combat can cast a cold and harsh light on these willing
gladiators with the fresh smiles and the twinkling
eyes. Growing up was to be accelerated for some and
extinguished for others.

Becoming a sophomore, or a Third Classman, was
a welcomed relief from the previous year. But it was
a year of transition for most. You weren't a Doolie
any more, but most of the responsibilities within the
squadron [and, hence, the privileges] fell on the
upper two classes. Third Classmen were not allowed to
wear civilian clothes or drink alcohol in public. Only
First Classmen owned cars, so getting about was always
a challenge. A Third Classman's dream was a girlfriend
with wheels, money, her own place and a good sense
of humor. More than once had Dave unfolded that
little piece of paper in his billfold. Maybe it was just his
horny imagination, but he still thought he could catch
the fragrance of Dawn's perfume.

The summer between the Doolie year and the
sophomore, or Thirdclass, year was their first
opportunity to leave the Academy since they first
entered a year earlier. It was a welcomed break and

significantly marked the end of the Doolie year and the beginning of the status and responsibility of being an upperclassman. When they returned at the end of the summer, a new Doolie class would be finishing its basic training and ready for their academic entry. Pete and Dave and their classmates would no longer be at the bottom of the totem pole...or the food chain.

The summer was short...lasting from the June graduation through the commencement of academics in mid-August. The class was required to tour military facilities throughout the US...including a week at the Army's Ft. Benning Jump School to learn as much as possible about parachuting as well as a week with the Navy. The balance of the stops on the tour were with Air Force units to expose the cadets to the "real Air Force"...whatever that was. Everyone used that phrase, but cadets at this level had little clue that the Academy was not reality. It was a wonderful time in their lives to be away from the Academy, to make better friends within their class, and to enjoy some encounters with civilians...especially those of the opposite sex. After all, they had been locked up for quite some time.

The experience with the US Navy out of Long Beach was one neither Pete nor Dave would ever forget. Pete drew the choicest assignment, an aircraft carrier. Dave initially was excited to be assigned to the USS Preston, a destroyer. He soon discovered though why they called it a destroyer, for it destroyed his stomach. He was sea sick from an hour after they departed until their return. He really was interested in the ship's systems operations but could only remain inside the cramped quarters for about an hour at a time. He must

Glenn Coleman

have vomited twice a day for the entire trip. Although
he ate Saltines continuously, he just could not get over
the pukes. He would have given a month's pay to be
back on Terra Firma, preferably walking the foothills
of the Bitterroots.

The Preston's duty within the carrier group was to
protect the carrier from submarines and to recover
downed aircrews if they missed the carrier on landing.
Carriers do not circle back to pluck pilots out of the
ocean. Dave was especially impressed by the submarine
detecting capabilities of the Preston...especially the
skill of the sonar operators, who claimed they could
determine the gender of the Humpbacks by the
impact of their strokes.

On the afternoon of the fifth day at sea, the Preston
came along side the carrier to refuel. The carrier
looked larger than Long Beach to the Preston swabbies
as they paralleled course at 20 knots about 200 feet
apart. The normal position for the Preston during
aircraft launch and recovery was a mile to the rear of
the carrier and a quarter mile to port. Pilot lines were
fired from the carrier across the destroyer. These were
used to draw the refueling hoses on board. Dave was
on the Preston's bridge when the XO handed Dave the
phone. "Somebody named Benedetto wants to talk to
you from the carrier, Dave. Anybody you know?"

"Yes, sir. My roommate." Dave hadn't talked to Pete
for almost a week and really didn't want to tell him
about the sea sickness. Dave bastardized one of
General Douglas MacArthur's famous quotations,
"From the bridge of the USS Preston, I send you one

single thought, one sole idea, written in puke on every beachhead from Australia to Tokyo. There is no substitute for solid ground…that doesn't pitch and roll. I gotta get off this tin can."

"Are you kidding me? queried Pete. "This carrier doesn't even move. You can't tell that we're even in the water."

"Look at us. We're bouncing around like a cork in the rapids over here. Even the inside of my stomach is green."

"Yeah, I can see you there on the bridge through these king-sized binoculars. Can you see me, Dave? I'm waving."

It was like looking at Manhattan from Newark. "Pete, I have no clue where you are. That carrier is huge."

"Sorry you're not feeling too cool, dude, but only two days to go…then a night in Long Beach. Want to get a tattoo?"

"Think I'll pass on the tattoo, but if you feel that sorry for me, trade places with me. I'm sleeping strapped in a bunk stacked three high. We get a gallon a day to shower. And all I've had to eat are a couple boxes of Saltines. This ride is killing me. I don't think I'll ever get used to it."

"Well, if you want to come over here, the Captain says it's okay. We're even going to launch off this boat in an S2F later today…and then we'll come back and land."

"Just how does one get from here to there? I'm sure as hell not swimming."

"It's easy. They strap you in a little swing with a pulley on it and pull you across on one of these lines that are stretched between these two boats…I mean ships."

"Yeah, right. See you in Long Beach, asshole."

"Ciao, amigo. Last one on the pier buys the first beer. See you there."

* * *

When Dave finally stepped off the ramp onto the pier at Long Beach, he wanted to get down and kiss the ground, but then he knew he had already looked pretty much like a dork to these swabbies. Tradition was on the ship that if you puked over the rail, then you had to clean it up…and every time he did, there was someone standing behind him with a mop and bucket ready to hand it to him. All in all, he was glad to have this behind him. "What's wrong with me?" he thought. "I've never been sea sick before…but then I've never been on a ship before, either."

Dave had been at sea for almost a week and was getting accustomed to the roll of the ship…getting your "sea legs" as one old CPO told him. What was so strange now that he was on solid ground was that the street beneath him seemed to be swaying. He noticed that the others leaving the ship seemed to be weaving and wobbling a bit as they walked down the street. "Edwards, take a note", he said to himself. "Fly through the clouds. Walk on the ground. But leave the big boats to the anchor-clankers!"

* * *

11

The summer had been good to both Pete and Dave.
They learned a lot and experienced much, but they
arrived back at the Academy with ten days to kill
before they were required to sign in and start the fall
academic semester. The new Doolies of the next class
were still in their summer training program, and the
upper two classes really did not want the new Third
Classmen around until the summer training was over.
They were free to take leave or stay at the Academy…
but away from the summer training programs.
Dave toyed with the idea of making it back north to
Montana. Pete had no interest in returning to Philly.

"Tell you what, Pete. Let's hitchhike back up to the Big
Sky country, and I'll show you living in the mountains.
You'll like it."

"I'm in, but what do you think about staying right
here. I hear the most beautiful part of Colorado is
right out our back door. We could head up Deadman's
Canyon and over to where we had survival training last
summer."

"Yeah, then we could make it down the Rampart Range
to Stanley Reservoir and spend some time fishing.
I hear the fishing's good, and I'll show you how to
clean and cook fish."

"Just like Lewis and Clark. That's cool with me."

That afternoon, they checked out a couple of bed rolls,
two ponchos, two canteens, a backpack for Pete and a
few other necessities from Cadet Supply. Dave still had
his uncle's old WWII backpack stashed in the squadron
storage room. They stopped by the cadet dining hall
to con Chief Dodge out of some grub for the trek.
He sent them along with a couple of loaves of bread
and two sticks of pepperoni. That didn't worry Dave
much, for this was summer in the Rockies, and game
was plentiful and the mountain onions and potatoes
were flowering. Pete held visions of eating a squirrel or
chewing on pine nuts. But Dave assured him of better
days. Pete again muttered to himself, "Just like Lewis
and Clark." He'd read the book.

* * *

The hike up Deadman's took about two hours along
a clearly marked and well-traveled path. The view
from two thousand feet above the Academy was
magnificent. Pete figured he could see all the way
across the Colorado plains into Kansas. The curvature
of the Earth was so evident; he wondered how anyone
could have ever imagined that the Earth was flat.
Below him were the twin towers of Cathedral Rock
and to the south, Colorado Springs and Pike's Peak.
He was looking down on the traffic at the Academy

landing strip at the base of Pine Valley that on this day included light airplanes, sail planes and parachutists. Everything seemed so small and insignificant from atop the Front Range. Even the Cadet Area paled relative to the magnitude of the mountains. Pete reflected on how small even one life was in the great cogged gear train called <u>life</u>. The prominence of the Rockies can do that. He felt that recurring urge to write his poetry, but there was no time for that right now. The thoughts in his mind and the passions in his heart would have to wait.

Three more hours of fairly easy hiking brought Dave and Pete into a beautiful high meadow with abundant water, perfect for setting up camp for the night. Although they were on no set schedule, when night falls in the mountains, it comes swiftly, and the work must be finished. The nearest streetlights or porch lights were six or seven miles away and several thousand feet below. The gathering of firewood and the setting of camp are daylight chores and necessities. The mountains were still damp from the spring rains so a good campfire was at the top of their list. There is something about a campfire to make a meadow a home. While neither Dave nor Pete had a recipe for campfire pepperoni, it did provide some light and warmth, and a false feeling of security. And the smoke tended to keep the flying critters at bay. And there is nothing better than a hot cup of campfire coffee on a cool and crisp night in the Front Range.

It's a magic time to lay by the fire and watch the stars come out one at a time. The last flicker of the daylight fades as the eyes become more and more accustomed

to the darkness. It is a 30-minute adventure that every
mountain traveler has experienced and honors. It is
a time to be quiet and to marvel at God's majesty. On
this night, Mars was the first to appear, with its red
glow, followed by what Dave thought was Jupiter. He
pulled out his binoculars and could barely make out its
moons, just as Galileo has done centuries before. And
then the stars in Orion's belt appeared. Dave always
called Orion the skier's constellation, for it was always
high in the winter's sky and could only be seen now,
because of the Earth's position in its orbit around the
sun, in the early evening near the horizon. "If you are
ever going to navigate at night, Orion is an easy group
to find, and his head always points east and his sword
west," Dave told Pete.

"Well, did you know that the word <u>planet</u> is derived
from an ancient Greek word that means wanderer,
for while the stars like Polaris and those that make up
Orion's belt stay in their same position relative to each
other, the planets like Mars and Jupiter travel in their
own orbit across the backdrop of the stars?" countered
Pete. "I used to date a girl in Philly who worked in the
planetarium and sat through her presentation too
many times." He pointed out Polaris, the north star,
and how to use the Big Dipper or the W to find it.

The full moon would be coming up soon, and the glow
would blind them to over half of the stars they could
now see. Dave spoke of someday traveling through
space and being that pinpoint of light moving across
the night sky and perhaps being identified by campers
in this very meadow…just as they may have done
Sputnik years before. Dave, like Pete, was a dreamer…

and there was no better time or place than here and now. The mountains can do that to the receptive mind.

"Dave, I know you are used to all this...the mountains, the crisp air, the stars, the smell of the pines. But to me, this is absolute heaven. It is so far from where I came from in Philly. You just cannot imagine. If I went back home tomorrow and tried to explain this to all my buddies, they wouldn't understand what I was talking about. I would be speaking another language. They'd nod their heads and go back to talking about the Eagles and Buddy Ryan...and Dick Clark. They just wouldn't get it. I am one lucky dude to be given another chance at life...this life."

"You ain't wrong, brother. This is good living. I hope I never leave the mountains...but I know I will have to in this business. But my heart will always be right here. Every time I see a full moon rising, I will always think about the clear night sky in the Rockies...and the Bitterroots. I really had to think about it, leaving the mountains, when I decided to come here, because I know we are going to see the world. But as my old fishing buddy told me, every time you turn right, something is left. Billy was just a cow poke, but he was pretty smart."

The campfire was down to embers now...and the conversation slowed. Pete and Dave each turned in to themselves and their own thoughts as their brains retreated from the events of the day and the physical exertion of the hike. Pete had wanted to write down his thoughts all day. It had been that kind of a day. And that was his last thought as he succumbed to a good night's sleep under the stars.

* * *

Custom dictates that the first one to rise starts the
fire and boils the water for coffee. One might think
that feigning sleep until the other gets up would be
the smart route to take…but not in the Rockies and
not with these two. When that first sunlight comes
across Kansas at over a thousand miles an hour and
first catches the tops of the Rockies, most mountain
folks are happy to be there and be part of it. The
plains down below are still bathed in the darkness, but
daylight on the mountain top is always greeted with
delight. It's time to shake the critters out of your boots
and think of the dozen reasons why not to shave.

Dave had wisely gathered firewood the afternoon
before and had it burning before Pete returned
from the creek with a #10 can full of water. Drinking
straight from the creek was probably safe, but one
never knows what is just upstream. Boiling the water
takes care of most sins and delays the diarrhea to
a more appropriate time. Water boils at such a low
temperature at this altitude, so the allure of campfire
coffee is more in the mind than in the mouth. But it's
still a wonderful way to clear the head and ease the
pain of sleeping on the ground. Neither Dave nor Pete
cared much for breakfast but figured a few carbs would
help making it through the day. So a couple slices of
white bread toasted over the fire on a stick and a bit of
peanut butter would have to do.

A couple of cans of water took care of the fire, and
Dave covered what was left with dirt. A change of
underwear and socks, and they were ready to head

for the next checkpoint, a five-hour hike to the south. Moving west from the Front Range a few miles took them away from the deepest canyons and provided for fewer contour lines on the map. That converts to less climbing and easier hiking. The down side of staying high is that you are away from water. Their goal was to be at the Stanley Canyon beaver ponds before dark so that Dave could get in a bit of fishing for their dinner.

Noon found Lewis and Clark hiking south down a jeep trail with only a few swallows left in their canteens. They weren't in a critical situation yet, but the thought of water was certainly on their minds. They had not seen anyone else since they had left their meadow campsite, so to round the corner and encounter a Jeep was quite a surprise to both Dave and Pete…as well as to the guy and gal in the Jeep.

The Jeep was sitting high center atop a large boulder in the trail. The driver appeared to be digging at the boulder. His passenger was sitting in her seat with an annoyed look on her face. Both seemed quite out of place in the mountains in a Jeep off the main road.

"Hey," greeted Dave. "Got a problem?"

"I think I'm stuck. I'm trying to get this rock out of the way."

Dave and Pete looked at each other and just smiled. "Rookie," Dave mumbled under his breath. When it's the shovel against the boulder, the boulder always wins. And they couldn't help but notice his passenger in her cutoff jeans and tank top. She obviously wasn't dressed for the mountains, but for two guys who attended a military school, she looked damned good…but not as good as the cooler in the back seat of the Jeep.

"Think you could help me get this rock out of the way?" he asked.

"Well, that depends on what you got in your cooler. I think we can work out a trade." The girl must have found that amusing as she smiled, leaned provocatively over the seat and opened the lid. The cooler was filled with green barrel-shaped bottles of beer. Dave amused himself by the thought that if he had to choose between this cutie and her cold beer, right now he'd go with the beer. "Maybe," he thought, "I've been hanging out with the guys too much." She took out two, dried them off slowly on her tank top, pitched one over to Pete, and the other to Dave, who sat down on a boulder to enjoy the beer…and the tank top. This may have been the best beer Dave had ever had…and he'd had a few.

Dave took his time enjoying his beer and the scenery. He knew he was cutting into their plans, but right now, he held all the cards and wasn't in a rush to change anything. Finally, Dave took the jack off the back of the Jeep and raised the right side of the Jeep. He stacked smaller boulders under both wheels and let it down. Then he climbed under the wheel and drove the Jeep down the trail a few feet. He grabbed two more beers, picked up his old khaki backpack and headed south once more. "Come on, Pete. I hear fish calling my name." He couldn't help himself from looking back to see if she were looking back…and she was.

* * *

Their day's trek took them from north to south along the Front Range, about four or five miles west of the Academy site…but several thousand feet about it. They followed Jeep trails when they could, for these trails were generally smoother and flatter. But sometimes it was just better to cut across some of the shallower canyons where a vehicle couldn't go. They were trying to make it to a place called Farish Memorial, a mountain lake and cabins donated to the Academy by the parents of a Lt. Farish, a deceased Air Force pilot, to be used as a recreation area by the cadets. It lay in a beautiful mountain valley with camp sites and an old deserted ski run. Although they had never been up there during their Doolie year, they had heard stories of it from the upper class and were not disappointed when they entered the grounds protected by several huge boulders. It was breath-taking. But equaling the splendor was the joy of finding cool, fresh drinking water that didn't require boiling and a real porcelain crapper with real TP. Ah, the joy of simple living and living simple.

The small store there offered some candy items and snacks as well as some basic items such as batteries, matches and duct tape. Why duct tape? But the thing that caught Dave's eye was fish bait. "Fishing any good here?" he asked the girl behind the counter.

"Depends on what you boys are fishing for," she said with a wink of her eye so obviously aimed at Pete. Her name was Barb and, for this summer, she ran the facility.

Pete was always amused at the mountain girls, how they flirted, how they dressed...or didn't. "I'm a long way from South Philly," he muttered to himself. "And I'm liking it."

Dave wanted to try his luck in this lake, and it was getting later than they had planned. So Pete and Dave decided to end the day's trek there at Farish and head for Stanley the next day. To continue would put them on the trail after dark, and trekking at night is always a challenge...especially in new territory and especially in the mountains. Plus Dave had been bragging on the trail just how good his planked trout was...and hopefully, he will get to show it off with a good catch and a better dinner. And Pete was hoping to see a bit more of Barb.

They had their choice of camp sites for two dollars a night...and that included a real shower and yes, access to the porcelain crapper. Pete picked out a campsite near the lake and atop a small knoll. But the main reason was probably the large stack of firewood already assembled. It was a bit farther from the shower and the toilets, but those things seem to be more important to the ladies than to the guys.

There was a permanent fire pit, and in no time Pete had a hearty fire going for Dave's catch and to take the edge off the cool of the evening that was now setting in.

"Hey, you guys want some company?" Through the failing light, Pete could make out the outline of a girl carrying a sack and a blanket. It was Barb.

"What the hell," he thought. "A girl, a blanket, a cool night in the mountains with a good fire…and a sack. Well, three out of four ain't bad. Maybe she brought some brewski in the sack. I think I'm liking this outdoors life."

When Dave returned to the campsite with his catch, Pete and Barb were sitting on the blanket working on their first beers about as close to the fire and as close to each other as could be without something catching fire. Pete could feel the fire's heat through the brass rivets of his Levis. Sitting there so close to Barb was generating its own brand of heat that Barb also was so obviously feeling. It had been a long time for Pete. The life of a Doolie in the Academy's first year is Spartan in most of the important aspects. "Do I need to find another fire," asked Dave with a twinkle in his eye.

"Okay by me," said Pete.

"Sit down, stud fisherman, and start cleaning fish," added Barb, tossing Dave a cold one from her bag of tricks. Soon the filets were over the fire held by green, forked aspen sticks.

"Nothing but a little salt and a sprinkling of chili powder on these beauties…unless you got something in your poke," Dave queried.

"Just the basics of cooking in here, Dave…bread, some Oreos and, oh yes, a couple of six packs."

"Well, then, it looks like fish sandwiches tonight," announced Dave. "And pork'n'beans. I got a can of beans in my backpack…and some mountain onions

I picked last night. It ain't fancy, but we didn't know we were having such pleasant company for dinner." She acknowledged with a conjured shy smile, glancing over toward Pete.

After an adequate dinner and three beers at that altitude, Dave began to think about stretching out and bedding down. The Law of the Jungle would normally call for Dave to disappear and leave the fire to Pete and Barb, but this was Barb's turf, and she probably had better offerings…if any offering at all. It wasn't long before they disappeared from the campsite… without comment.

* * *

Sleeping under the stars in the mountains comes to an abrupt end when the sky brightens as it announces the return of the sun. The security and privacy provided by the cover of darkness give way to a feeling of nakedness in the daylight, and staying horizontal for Dave seemed somewhat lazy and exposed. He loved to wake up to the crisp mountain air and the way that it made his nostrils tingle. As his head shook off the night's sleep, he noticed three things obviously missing from the camp…a fire, hot coffee…and Pete. He felt a smile creeping up his face. "Hopefully," he thought, "there are two happier people in the world this morning." And he went fishing. And he thought of Dawn. He recalled her comments about local girls and cadets. She would have loved this place. He wondered whatever happened to her. He assumed that she and "Charlie" had married after Graduation two months earlier and were now out in the Air Force living the good life…probably at Pilot Training.

Within the hour, Pete came wandering around the lake heading for the campsite, looking like he'd been rode hard and put away wet. His grin answered all questions, and nothing else was said. After a hearty breakfast of coffee and jerky and a little hardtack, they doused the fire, broke camp and headed for Stanley Reservoir. Just when they were about to cross that last ridge and lose sight of Farish, Pete looked back to capture the memory. He thought he could see Barb standing next to the flagpole. He hoped she missed him as much as he was missing her. She didn't.

* * *

12

The hike from Farish to Stanley was an easy one, with
little change of altitude and Jeep trails that covered
most of the distance. It couldn't have been more than
four miles. Dave and Pete soon figured that the trail
had been well marked with blue plastic ribbons tied
to tree limbs every few hundred yards. They made
good time, and by noon, they were looking at the most
beautiful mountain reservoir Pete had ever imagined.
Just for a moment, Dave thought he was back home
in the Bitterroots. They chose a campsite atop a low
ridge next to the water…just as the Indians would have
done. There were many signs that others had camped
here before…a prepared fire pit, a stack of tree limbs
for fire wood and logs to sit on. Backpackers this far off
the beaten paths tend to leave clean camp sites…and
this was no exception. The Law of the Jungle required
that you leave a camp cleaner than you found it. The
Indians' code was to leave no sign that you had even
been there. Dave soon found several arrowheads and a
piece of broken pottery that proved that they had.

There was a lot of stuff going on in Pete's mind: the events back at Farish, the melancholy of several days in this mountain splendor, the survival of his first Academy year, the challenge of the upcoming academic year. Some days, Pete thought his mind would explode…but all in all, he knew he was in the right place and on the right track. He had needed this trek across the Front Range to put his house back in order and was in no hurry for it to end.

Pete looked forward to times like this, where he could think without reservations, where he could allow his defenses to wane and his imagination to run free. He had started a poem in his mind two nights before in that mountain high meadow, and it was getting too complex now not to get in down on paper. So he pulled his notebook from his pack and started to write. He wanted to write about himself and his feelings, but his encounter with Barb continued to get in the way. Sometimes the thin mountain air is a cheap drunk. Sometimes the brain visits its own dark corners spurred on by the lack of oxygen and the lack of outside stimuli. With Dave's hook in the water across the lake, now was a perfect time for reflection and creation. It's too bad that such quiet times needed to be scheduled. What kind of a life, Pete wondered, is this? He answered his own question out loud, "It's my life, and it is what it is. Deal with it, Benedetto."

Pete's dad had never said much of value to Pete while he was growing up. As far as that goes, he never said much to anyone. But the one bit of wisdom he shared with Pete was that while it was important to know what you know, it was often more important to know what

you don't know. And Pete always took that to heart...
and right now was a good time to stop and take account
of just what was going on in his life. He knew that he
didn't have any idea where his life was going to take
him, but that he was preparing himself in a fine fashion
for that unknown. He was preparing his body and his
mind for whatever came to him. He knew he was on a
journey with no knowledge of the destination. He knew
there was a fire in his gut but did not fully comprehend
the passion that filled him. But he lived with a solid
faith that his life was to count for something, that
he should reach for the sky and refuse to accept
anything less. It was not an arrogance, but rather a self-
confidence. As Dandy Don Meredith once said, "It ain't
braggin' if you can do it." He began to write:

Somewhere hidden in the depths of his spirit
Burned a fire to be free, really free.
The sparks lay dormant for these generations past,
Yet it flares now so vigorously.

This young man was of the lineage of Icarus,
His kinsman, Orion, the brave,
The call was for mastery of heavens,
And in victory, he became a slave.

His friend, Douhet, so aptly noted
How differences did abound.
We are a new breed of cat, we fly through the air
While others set roots to the ground.

Too often mankind decides to be blind.
We pick a lesser path.
We knowingly waste a given talent.
We invite the Master's wrath.

Yet this young man was the slave of perfection.
"Towards Excellence" became his creed.
He had no regard for the scorecard of others.
Acclaim was not of his need.

The pursuit of glory created no pressures.
His drive was alive from within.
He was his judge as well as his jury.
He was his own best friend.

Goals were set and goals were met,
And he was never surprised.
One seldom exceeds his own expectations.
He expected to reach the skies.

He looked on himself and he liked what he saw
Through critical yet sensitive eyes.
Ego be damned, I know what I am,
Productive, self-confident and wise.

Fame and glory generally come
To those who reach so high,
But glory is fleeting and fame is shallow,
And they seldom satisfy.

Wisdom, excellence and self-esteem
Always come hand-in-hand.
They are qualities left in us by our Master
To develop as best we can.

As he grew older, he also grew bolder,
His excellence, no limits knew.
He reached for the skies and conquered.
How kudos did accrue.

He enters now onto the hallowed page
With name indelibly scribed
Twixt laws of nature and heroes of yore,
Forever his spirit to reside.

As this world turns and the seasons change,
Some disciplines must hold fast.
His strength provides our guiding light.
Long shadows have been cast.

So he joins now Douhet and Icarus,
Standing proudly with Orion, the brave.
Entering the pages of agelessness,
On tables of stone to engrave.

He knows this page most recently written
Will pass from father to son.
Long shadows are cast, yet he joins the past
Knowing battle with future is won.

His successes and victories and triumphs
Now have satisfied his own mind.
But the greatest treasure he owns forever
Is what he has left behind.

"My God", thought Pete. "Have I just written my own
epitaph? Is my whole life just two pages long?" Pete
never questioned what he wrote, for he knew it came
from some source deep inside that he could neither
touch nor control. It just happened, and he never
edited nor retouched what came forward. Pete wanted
to do something marvelous with his life. To him, life
itself and the talents bestowed upon him were gifts
selected specifically for him by a God that he knew
existed but knew he didn't fully understand.

* * *

That night after another delicious meal of fish sandwiches and jerky, Pete was in the mood to revisit his afternoon's thoughts. He trusted Dave with his deepest feelings and concerns, and Dave had never let him down. Each one of their discussions of this type over this past year had taken them individually to new places and a higher understanding of life. And it had locked their friendship into an impregnable ring of trust and love. Pete's only brother was just a baby when he left home, so he never had a friend like Dave... about as close as a brother could be.

"Okay, Dave, the subject for the evening is...God. You first."

Dave had just lit his stubby little pipe...claimed it helped keep the mosquitoes away. They both knew there wasn't a mosquito within a hundred miles. Dave exercised his poker face and took another slow draw. "God, huh?"

"Yeah, God, like in..."

"I know. I know. I'm just wondering where that question came from...and how I'm going to answer it."

Another puff on the pipe as Dave stared into the fire. "I've spent most of my life in the beauty of these mountains. I respect the laws of nature as things are put together out here. I have seen magnificent elk. I have admired the beauty of the spider web and the trout. I have looked up into the heavens and counted stars until I fell asleep. I have seen child birth and have helped cows with their delivery. And I've seen new fawns that were still wet. I know this was all here long before me and that it will be here long after I'm gone. I know I, and you, are but small cogs in this process. This was no accident. This didn't result from some freak of nature. Something or somebody had to set all of this in motion. And I don't know who or what that was or is. But the Indians knew and saw the same things I have, and they believe in spirits and that there is somebody in charge of all of this. They don't know who, but they believe...and so do I. Who is God? I don't really know. Sometimes I think he sits next to me at the campfire. Other times, I think he has forgotten my name...maybe busy with someone else. But I know he loves me and he watches over me and he protects me as well as he can without taking away my freedom of choice. He's not responsible for some of the dumb things I do...but that's free will. He expects me to do right and to do what's right for his world here. I'm sure you have a better answer...or you would not have brought it up."

"Do you think he has a plan already in place for you? Is your future already decided upon and fixed? Does he have a wife and kids already picked out for you? Does he know when you are going to die?"

"Whoa, mule. You are getting way ahead of me. I think of God as the creator of all this. This is his gift to us. Life is his gift to us. He expects us to honor these gifts...to use our talents, to be good to others, to not mess the place up, to do the best we can do. I think he gives us a lot of rope to hang ourselves, and we'll have to answer for our shortcomings someday. He doesn't run our lives, but he has high hopes and expectations and hurts when we fail. But you know, most everybody falls short, so he must be pretty unhappy with us. Isn't that what Jonah and that flood was all about?"

"I'm pretty sure that it was Noah that had the flood. But do you think God knows our future?"

"No, I don't think so...well, maybe. I'm not so sure he even cares so much exactly how our future unfolds. He wires us up the way we are, hopes the best for us, and sets us free. He knows we will fail in many ways, but I don't think he knows where all of our decisions will take us. I think when he set us free that he knew what he was getting into. But that was his decision. I bet he laughs a lot at us...and cries a lot, too."

"What if you're wrong?"

"Well, I guess I won't know. When I die, I'm finished. And nobody gets out of here alive. But it comes down to this. I'd rather live a life believing in a God and be wrong than to live a life not believing. So really, I am a happier person believing in God. Maybe that's selfish and done for the wrong reason, but that's just the way I have grown up to feel. Believing in God just fits into how I understand life and everything around me. It is what it is...and maybe I'm wrong...but I don't think so."

Pete thought quietly on this and stared into the fire for what must have been too long a time for Dave's comfort. "Well?" Dave asked.

"Well, the whole Benedetto clan for generations has bought totally into this Catholic thing...Catholic school, mass every time the doors are open, Bingo, confession, guilt trips, whippings by the Mother Superior...the whole thing. So this is really the first time to have the freedom to think freely about what's real and what's liturgical bull shit. Yeah, I believe there is a God...one God. And I believe he put us here and put us here for a reason. And this is where I'm still searching for a reason. Like Chuck Yeager said, "This may not be the way it happened, but this is the way I want to remember it happened." And I may have it totally wrong, but I think God, in all his omnipotence, looked around at his creations and was missing something. He was a loving God and wanted to be loved in return. But there was nothing for him to be loved by. He needed something with a heart...a soul. So he created a universe that follows all the rules of nature and all the F=ma stuff, and then he created Man to love. But God, being very wise, realized that even though he could wire up Man to force him to love God, that wasn't the kind of love he was after. He wanted Man to be free to choose...to love or not to love. It was only if Man had a choice to make that it counted. When Man has the freedom to love or not to love...and then chooses to love...then it is really love. And that is what God wanted. So, just as you said, he wired us up that way, gave us free will, and is willing to accept the rejection if that is what Man does to him. God wants us to love him. God needs for us to love him. And it makes him sad if we don't. But he's not going to kill us if we don't. But he's going to reward us if we do."

"Pete, are we talking about heaven here?"

"Yeah, partially. But if we choose to love him, we also seem to lead a better life."

"May be, Pete, but good people suffer. They die young and broke. Where's the justice there?"

"I don't know…but I got a theory," offered Pete. God knows how great heaven is, and listen to this. He doesn't care when in your life you come to heaven. When he granted us free will, he made the choice to let us have some impact on when we die. We may drive too fast, smoke too much…"

"Or choose to fly airplanes for a living?" countered Dave.

"Right! He gives us free will to live and to love and to make choices. But he also listens to our prayers and needs. And always answers them."

"Always, Pete? I don't think so."

Pete continued with his philosophy. "He may not give us what we want or think we need. But he always gives us the wisdom to make a good choice. But it's our choice. That's the difference. He wants us to do right and to do good. But it's still our choice. That's why I think he sent Jesus. Before Jesus, everything was Jewish Law…all the shalls and shall nots. But that's not what God intended. It had gotten out of hand, and God wanted to get us back on track. He sent Jesus as a man to tell us about love, about loving ourselves and loving each other and loving God. That's where it all makes a circle. God wanted us and created us to love each other and to love God. He sent Jesus to tell us the story, and that's what he did. He hates war and all the stuff we do to each other."

"Do you think he hates warriors?"

"Huh?"

"Pete, do you think he hates those of us who choose war as a profession...like we are doing?"

"Dave, war may be our profession, but peace is our goal. I think God is a warrior, too. He's been fighting battles on our behalf since the very beginning of time. He's on the side of good...and so are we. You know, I think I feel another poem coming on."

"I think I feel a good night's sleep coming on. But I like what I hear on this God thing. I'm glad you brought it up. Altar Boy and Mountain Man are really not that far apart in their beliefs...especially the free will stuff."

Dave wasn't sure exactly when he went off to sleep, but he lay quietly on top of his mummy bag staring at the stars for a long time. With the high altitude and the limited pollution, the sky was quite clear. With his binoculars, he could still make out two of the four Galilean moons of Jupiter and watched as some satellite ripped across the motionless backdrop of the Milky Way. He recalled seeing Sputnik for the first time and the impact it had upon the world, how the adults talked of this being the end of the Western democracy. Well, men once thought all heavenly bodies orbited the Earth, too. Galileo had used his moons orbiting Jupiter to support his argument that since Jupiter had moons circling it, it was okay to have things orbiting other planets than Earth, that our planet was not necessarily the center of God's universe. Some of his day thought such thinking to be heresy, but history and science proved them to be wrong. And their being wrong never created much change nor had much impact.

Thoughts of the day and of the trip raced through his mind. Dave knew he was in a transition...somewhere between high school back in Montana and the rest of his life. This is a scary place for a young man to be. He leaves the comfort and organization and the stability of his home of all of his life thus far and moves toward a life of adventure, relationships, maybe marriage and children. He had come a long way but knew he had just begun the trip. Just like Pete's dad had said, he knew what he knew and knew that there was a lot he didn't know. But for the right now, he was glad to be where he was, with his friend, Pete, next to a lake full of fish just waiting to be had. Tomorrow would be another good day.

* * *

13

Pete always knew when he was waking up from a good sleep, for the thoughts running through were more than dreams. They were complex thoughts that required decisions and actions. This was when he knew it was time to get up. The chances of his going back to sleep were nil.

Stanley Reservoir was covered in a fog that occurs whenever the wind is light and out of the east. The breeze from the plains pushes any moisture up the Front Range, cooling it and condensing that moisture into clouds…and their earth-bound twin, fog. On mornings like these, he always thought of Longfellow's opening line from <u>Evangeline</u>…"This is the forest primeval…"

Off in the distance, he heard someone whistling Colonel Bogey's March from <u>The Bridge on the River Kwai</u>. He knew it wasn't Dave, for he would be fishing by now, and that kind of noise would scare the fish. As the music drew closer, he could make out through the fog the outline of a man carrying fishing gear. "Good morning, how's the fishing?"

"Don't know. You"ll have to ask my buddy, Dave, there across the lake. I'm sure he's been up long enough to know. I'm about to brew up some coffee. Would you like a cup?"

"Thanks, but I brought my own. But I might take on a refill a little later if you have any left."

"I'll be sure to save you some. By the way, where did you come from? Were you camping here last night? I didn't think there was anyone else around."

"Oh, I work down at the Academy. I teach Aero. I come up here to fish on the way to work some during the summer when the work is light. We're about to start the academic year again, so my fishing days are getting limited."

"I'm sorry. I guess I should be addressing you as "sir". Dave and I are cadets and are about to start our second year. Pete's my name, sir."

"Oh, save the sir crap for later. Up here, we are just fishing...and drinking coffee. I graduated there myself eleven years ago. Now I'm back here teaching Aero and doing a little flight instruction on the side. Roger's the name," as he stuck out his hand to Pete.

"Pete...Pete Benedetto. Glad to meet you. And that's Dave Edwards over there. We are up here for one last outing before school starts next week...kinda like you in that regard, sir."

Roger rolled his eyes. "Sorry, Roger, some habits are hard to break...sir." They both smiled. There is a bond among those who survive an academy system. It's not unlike combat or sex in that you cannot truly explain it to anyone who hasn't personally been through it. The adjectives just do not exist in the English language. Still, the silent bond draws brother to brother.

This pastoral moment was abruptly interrupted by the wild squawking of a duck in flight. An eagle had just made a pass on him, ripping loose a few of his feathers. As the eagle circled around for the final kill, the duck flew down just above the water. And just as the eagle was about to make his kill, the duck folded his wings and plunged head first into the lake. The eagle was committed to take his prey and couldn't prevent hitting the water also. Eagles are great at plucking fish out of the water, but they are not good swimmers...nor do they particularly like the water. The eagle struggled to get airborne again and staggered back into the air where they are master. Finally the duck resurfaced and squawked loudly at the departing and dripping eagle in what must have meant "fuck you" in duck talk.

Roger and Pete watched with their mouths ajar. Neither had ever seen such an encounter. "Duck 1; Eagle 0. Must be a lesson in there somewhere," mused Pete.

Roger headed on around the lake to meet Dave and wet a hook next to his.

Pete's morning was spent reflecting on his latest poem and just whittlin' on a stick. A fellow can kill a lot of time and add a lot of value to his life with a sharp knife and a stick. Heck, even wisdom can be found sometimes. About mid-morning, Roger hollered at him as he headed back down the canyon toward his work. He never did get that second cup of coffee and was probably better off for it. Campfire coffee always sounds more enticing than it ever is. A solid piece in a cup of homemade coffee is usually coffee...where from the campfire, it could be ashes, dirt or horsefly dung.

As Roger disappeared through the tall grass at the mouth of the canyon, Pete decided to climb the ridge to the northeast to check if he could see the Academy. He had heard a cargo plane had crashed up there years earlier and thought he might just stumble into something interesting.

Two hours of hiking failed to turn up the airplane wreckage, but he did find a point where he could see the Cadet Area and the plains out to the east of Colorado Springs. He was about two thousand feet above the Valley Highway that ran from the Springs up to Denver and figured he could probably see all the way into Kansas. And of course, he had failed to bring his camera, but he added some beautiful vistas into the collection he always kept filed in his mind.

He was even higher than the traffic pattern at Peterson Field where he landed when he first came to Colorado a little over a year ago. As he watched an airliner shoot its approach to landing, he reflected on his thoughts of that particular day, how he had vowed to start his life again and in a new direction. He was happy with the results of his first Academy year and held in his heart that same fire and conviction. Pete still did not know where his life was going, but he was loving the journey. He knew there were things he didn't know but accepted that as part of the trip.

As the shadows of the Front Range began to stretch eastward first over the foothills, then over the Academy Airfield and South Gate, Pete figured it to be time to head back to Stanley Reservoir and camp. Dave had taught Pete to always stop and look over his shoulder when backpacking, for things look different when you are coming back in the opposite direction. Pete figured he had a couple hours of good light left when he once again hit the jeep trail they had taken from Farish to Stanley. He paused but for a moment as he was tempted to turn right and head back for another encounter with Barb. "Fish sandwiches and jerky… or Barb?" he muttered aloud. He could still smell her perfume on his shirt. A reluctant left turn and thirty minutes brought him back to Dave's campfire…and fresh fish sandwiches.

This would be their last night in the mountains for a while, and neither really wanted to give up the day. But the meal was finished and the mess kits were cleaned and the fire began to dwindle. The coffee did taste good if you saturated it with sugar. Yet even with the doses of caffeine and sugar, Pete and Dave were quiet and tranquil. It had been a good and beneficial outing for both. Tomorrow would bring this freedom to an end, and another academic year would begin. They were ready. Their coping tools had been sharpened. Bring it on.

* * *

Dave arose earlier than Pete and had failed to build a fire, even though they had gathered wood for it the previous day. "I just didn't feel like it. I know what lies before us, and I want to get started." Not much was said as they broke camp. They poured water on the fire pit and stirred it around to ensure it was totally out. Then Pete laid good wood next to it for the next camper. There was no policing up necessary since they regularly kept their campsites orderly.

They had seen Roger head for the tall grass and started in that direction. They knew the creek coming out of Stanley Reservoir had to go to the mouth of the canyon and followed it. Soon the trail started steeply downward.

The canyon was deep and filled with large boulders. The sounds of the rushing waters coupled with the wind rustling through the trees were significant. Pete and Dave picked their steps carefully just as the many hikers that had used this trail must have done. Dave thought of the Indians of hundreds of years previous who had made this journey in search of game or perhaps relief from the summer heat on the plains below. Where there was room, the trail was obvious and wide.

About an hour into the trek, they came upon a small cabin built right next to the trail...hardly large enough for a man to lie down in. From the looks of its construction and the lack of hardware at its door, it must have dated back over a hundred years. They wondered about its origin...perhaps a trapper's cabin or just a resting spot for hikers or perhaps shelter from the Front Range storms. Pete vowed to return to spend the night there and could feel the welcoming presence of its past.

Just beyond the mystical cabin, they came to a wide spot in the trail where someone had built a low wall perhaps to protect hikers from the deep canyon below. Pete and Dave knew from Roger's comments that this would be about half way back to the Academy and were ready to take a break. They dropped their packs on the ground and sat leaning against the wall. They finished their canteens with a bit of jerky since their trek was nearing its end.

"Dave, have you ever had the feeling you have been some place before? Well, I'm having one of those right now. There's something about this very spot. Maybe in an earlier life I was a trapper working this area...or maybe a gold prospector."

"Naw, you were probably an Indian...Dripping Peter, brave chief of the Pepperoni tribe. And instead of feathers, you probably wore a large pinky ring."

"Screw you, plow boy."

"Wait, just for a moment, you sounded just like Stebinski."

"And screw the horse you rode into town on."

When they finally emerged from the bottom of the canyon, they turned north to follow the power lines back to the Cadet Area. Things were beginning to look more familiar now...for better or for worse. This magnificent journey had ended, but the lessons learned and the events encountered had changed each of them in unique ways.

* * *

14

The Air Force Academy, like any other academy, looks different to an upperclassman than it does to a Doolie. Gone now are the double-timing everywhere, square corners, eyes straight ahead, limited meals sitting on the front edge of your chair, and memorizing knowledge such as famous quotations, military trivia and chains of command. Upon Recognition as an upperclassman, the cadet is free from the Fourth Class system with all of its stress and strain. Trips to class or to the john are at leisure. Casual conversation in public is finally allowed. In short, upperclassmen are allowed to be real people as much as cadets are allowed to be…but that's another story.

Yet Third Classmen, such as Pete and Dave, were still in cadet purgatory, an informal suspension between being a know-nothing, dirtbag Doolie and a fully respected and privileged Firstie or Second Classman. They were no longer the bottom of the food chain since they had a new Doolie class under them, yet they were not fully accepted by their upper class, those who only weeks before considered them, by all evidence, to be totally worthless and should be eradicated from the Cadet Wing and the face of the earth. My, how things had changed with Recognition.

Both Pete and Dave were comfortable in their abilities...not overly proud, but comfortable. They both were highly competitive and equipped for the competition that the Academy required. And they each had the faith in themselves to know where they stood in this Long Blue Line. A year earlier, on their second day as a cadet, they sat with their entire class in a huge lecture hall in Fairchild Hall. The speaker, the Dean of the Faculty, asked everyone in the room to stand up if they had been Valedictorian or Salutatorian of their high school graduating class. Pete and Dave both proudly popped up...only to find that about 90% of the rest of the room were also standing. The Dean then asked for all Eagle Scouts to stand, then captains of sports teams, then class officers, then those who had lettered in more than two sports, then... Well, it was a long list, and the results were uniformly significant. The message was clear. You are no longer in high school. There is no free ride. Each was competing with the best America could provide. And odds were that the person sitting to your right or to your left...or perhaps you...would not be there at graduation four years later.

Any military academy has the similar challenge to take this high-quality raw material, challenge it to its max, provide outstanding academic, military and physical training, and provide America and its military the finest for its leadership. Every minute of the cadet's day was battled for among the Dean, the Commandant and the Director of Athletics. Eight hours was reserved for a good night's sleep, but the rest of the day was a war zone, and the cadet was the victim, and often the wounded. It took eight hours of sleep and 6000 calories a day to keep these machines running proficiently at this speed. But it all seemed to work. History had already shown that if an American youth came to the Academy with a well adjusted personality and ego, they would graduate as a well adjusted, highly trained officer capable of immediate leadership capabilities. However, if one brought along baggage, such as an inflated ego or self-image or a chink in their personality, four years of maturation of this flaw produced some very interesting characters.

And the challenge to keep such inquisitive and innovative minds in wrap and occupied too often failed. Cadets always seemed to find the time and opportunity to pursue the bizarre. For example, it was a tradition within Pete's squadron to pass down each year to a new Third Classman the wrench that opened the fire hydrants that skirted the Terrazzo, the formation area just outside the dorm. The plan was to wait for the right opportunity to open hydrants and flood the formation area. That opportunity occurred on a Friday night in late January when the temperature was forecast to be in the teens. The Cadet Wing was scheduled for an In-Ranks Inspection and Parade the following morning. The entire Cadet Wing would be in place in full Parade Dress with hundreds of spectators viewing the regalia. Pete's plan was to sneak out of the dorm about midnight dressed in his dark blue warm-ups, avoid the Officer-in-Charge and his Security Flight, and get the hydrant open. The plan went without a hitch. In fact, Pete figured if one hydrant was good, two would be better and three, best. At best, he figured, the OIC or someone on Security Flight would spot the water and have it shut off. Pete and Dave were amazed at Reveille the next morning to find the hydrants still open and about twenty acres of six-inch thick ice that would not totally melt away until late March. Needless to say, the Commandant and his OIC were pissed and dictated that the Parade would go on as scheduled. The cadets would not win this one. Only after several dozen cadets had fallen just getting into their squadron formations did the Comm recant. His typical reaction was to restrict the entire Cadet Wing for the week-end…and he did. Cadets 1; Commandant 0.

There was a continuing challenge to come up with something just a little more bizarre than before. Picking up the OIC's car and depositing it in the Air Garden or some other "impossible" task became the mundane. The display aircraft that line the Terrazzo were always getting moved into some area that took a crane or disassembly to remove. Any task that required lots of willing laborers was fair game, but became boring. So someone would create a challenge to see who could do it first and best. The challenge usually went out in an underground newspaper called the Phoenix that somehow permeated the Cadet Wing weekly…usually on Tuesday nights. This was a read-and-destroy document that only got to the Commandant when it was to the cadets' advantage for him to know. Such was the competition to get a trash can on top of the flagpole. Now this was no normal flagpole. This is the kind you can see from miles away, the kind that you normally find only at car dealerships or fancy furniture stores. The challenge was to hang one of the large outdoor trash cans inverted on top of the flag pole. Some competitors thought about climbing the pole and pulling the can up after them. Some even toyed with the idea of a robot helicopter flying the can into position. The winner took the simplest of approaches. Late one moonless night after Taps, this team of four built an eight-foot long pole out of three hockey sticks and some duct tape. They then taped the middle of the long pole to the flag rope and then the bottom to the rope, with several loops around the pole to keep the stick vertical. They then placed the trash can inverted on top of the hockey sticks, hoisted the can up the pole until it was above the ball at the top of the pole, and then lowered the rope, hanging the can atop the pole. Then they disassembled it all and ran like hell. They must have been filled with pride when at the next morning's Breakfast Formation, the entire Cadet Wing broke out in applause. Each squadron formation gave an Eyes Right as they passed the pole en route to Mitchell Hall and breakfast.

Such shenanigans would, of course, require repair or return to the norm...and this was no different. The simple solution was to allow the cadets to 'fix it'. But no one was willing to risk injury to any cadet. They could beat their brains out in the boxing ring, jump out of perfectly good airplanes or have firing pins in their rifles. But someone else had to be retained to 'fix it'. So typically what would happen was to have some crane or tractor or paint team or whatever to come in for the repair…and then the bill was passed on to the Cadet Wing. At lunch, each cadet would be asked to ante up a dime or a quarter to pay for their spirit. It was generally money well spent.

And cadets would bet on anything. There were always football pools, pools on which new Doolie in the squadron would get laid first, pools of who would get the ugliest blind date at one of the Arnold Hall tea dances, and oh yes, the toilet paper races. In each latrine, there were six toilet stalls. Each of the six competitors would put a new roll of toilet paper on the roller, stick one end in the water in the toilet, and when all bets were down, would start flushing as quickly as possible. The first to empty the roll was declared the winner. Gambling was against the regulations, but it was another rule that was mostly ignored in the name of R&R.

One thing that the Commandant never seemed to learn [or maybe he did] was that to forbid cadets from doing something would almost ensure that it would be done. A case in point: the construction of the Cadet Chapel encountered many set-backs. The roof continued to leak. Parts would not fit properly. One problem followed another. One delay followed another. It became a source of jokes among the cadets. The Commandant laid down the edict that 'jokes about the Chapel were no longer funny'. The Cadet Wing, through its underground newspaper, responded with cartoons showing a chapel with a coin slot on the side and another with the hinged top swinging back to expose ICBM missiles ready for launch. Banners of all sorts would appear on the exposed girders. One Texas cadet even hung his state's flag from the very top of the northern-most spire. The construction workers removed it a week later with no bill.

Needless to say, life as a cadet could be a bit weird. Too many spend too much time with each other. Being sequestered in such an environment had its pros and its cons. One of the cons was the strange sense of humor the cadet developed just to maintain sanity. Yet properly channeled, this weirdness allowed and required cadets to challenge all edges of the envelope, accept nothing as absolute truth, and live on the outside of the box looking in. And that's not all a bad thing.

There was always a fine line between weirdness and creativity. Pete and Dave were no different and found unique ways to entertain and occupy themselves outside of the academics and militaria. One such experiment was a spin-off of the old game of gossip. One would start a rumor, telling the other of the precise time of launch, and the other would report back when he thought he had heard it. Normally it didn't take very long. Communications through this canned society was swift…though not always so accurate.

Another game they invented was called TOGWAR, The Original Game Without Any Rules…although it did have one rule out of the necessity to define the game. One would offer up a word or phrase…noun, verb, adjective or adverb…maybe a name or a place… it didn't matter. The other would then counter with another word that was connected in some hidden or vague manner. It was a battle of minutia and trivia. For example, Dave offered the word <u>two</u>. Several days later, Pete countered with <u>Samuel Clemens</u>. The connection was that Clemens, who spent much of his early life on the Mississippi river boats, wrote under the pen name of Mark Twain, and mark twain was a phrase used on the river boats meaning two fathoms of water, the minimum depth for safe clearance. Twain is an archaic word meaning two. Dave lost that battle and accepted defeat after a couple of days. Dave then countered with Charlie Gibson. Pete immediately drew the connection between Mark Twain's Tom Sawyer and Charlie Gibson's Diane Sawyer. He then countered with Firebird, the 60s era Gibson guitar. This unending game of trivia continued back and forth for all four years at the Academy, and although some of the connections were heavily disputed by one or the other, they ended their final game on the night before Graduation pretty much tied.

And finally, perhaps still reigning as the ultimate in weirdness and poor taste, Pete and Dave claimed ownership to the ruse and the naming of the Barf Lunch. Here, they took advantage of the inexperience of the Doolies on plane trips. Quite often, the entire Cadet Wing, or perhaps just large groups of them, would travel via C-130 transport aircraft to events such as football games or an inauguration. Generally, seating was in cramped side-by-side and knee-to-knee troop seating that ran the length of the aircraft. The Academy would send each cadet with a box lunch containing two half-pints of milk, a piece of fruit, a sandwich, a boiled egg, a candy bar, napkin and, of course, the infamous sick sack or barf bag. An hour or so after take-off when everyone was suffering from the stench of the old planes and older milk and even more cranky from the crowded and uncomfortable seating, Pete would empty one of his milks discretely into his sick sack and then start complaining about getting airsick. Then he would feign getting actively airsick [AKA puking] and, in a most disgusting manner, pretend to be filling the sick sack. He would wipe his mouth with his sleeve and tie off the top of the bag. Then he would look around as if looking for something to do with the sack. He would then call to Dave, who would be sitting some distance away, and pass the filled sack from cadet to cadet down to Dave. Everyone would handle it gingerly, even those who had seen it done before. Eventually, it would get to Dave, who would untie it, look into the sack, and then drink the contents of the bag. This whole scam would always claim a few greenhorn victims...the record being thirteen actively airsick cadets, all puking in unison. That always seemed to free up additional candy bars and sandwiches for the upperclassmen.

* * *

And so went the remainder of their stay at Camp USAFA, the Blue Zoo, Cloudland, Wild Blue U, the Rock...or whatever the favorite name was for that day. Every day was pretty much like any other day: Reveille, march to breakfast, class, march to lunch, class, intramurals, march to dinner, Call-to-Quarters [the required study time with no privileges or visiting], Tattoo and Taps. Saturdays could mean inspections and a parade. But Saturday afternoon through Sunday dinner was usually free, and if cadets had earned privileges through performance or seniority, they could take some time off from duties and the Academy. Having a girlfriend or knowing a Firstie with a car certainly helped. Yes, it was a weird life, but it was their life. And though they would never admit it, most seemed to love it and thrive in it. But the number that was always most important to each cadet was the ever-decreasing number of days to Graduation. And 100th Night was usually the mother of all parties. After that, figmosity reigned, and the focus was on getting the hell out of the Zoo and getting on with a real life.

* * *

15

Pete and Dave had both done very well in their four years at the Academy. Both had graduated in the top quarter of their class with a GPA of over 3.0. They each had been selected for leadership positions along the way and seemed to thrive under the additional challenges. Although the edge of the envelope seemed to be their normal hang-out, neither had suffered any permanent damage to their standings or reputation. It was just the reverse. Their attraction toward the bizarre often served as a magnet and an enticement for others to step out of the line and to get involved. Their adage was, "Do nothing, Say nothing, Be nothing." They instinctively tried to draw others out to also get involved. Others generally looked to them for leadership.

This trait was not uncommon at the Academy, and the military leadership wished they could replicate this gene in each of the cadets, for this was a trait so much needed in the military. But by being identified at cadet leaders, they were often invited by the Commandant to participate in appropriate Academy

functions. Dave and Pete often joked about how they
were just trained little puppets, on call at any time,
to perform for the visiting dignitaries. However, they
did get to meet some very interesting people, such as
Barry Goldwater, Sir Frank Whittle, Jimmy Doolittle
and Paul Garber.

Somewhere well hidden in the depths of their spirits,
each had a distinct love for the Academy. Although
neither would ever admit to it among their peers,
cadet life was to their liking. They loved the process
and the trip…but their focus was always on the
destination…albeit pretty much of an unknown.
Both wanted to fly and attacked such courses as Aero
Engineering, Physics, Navigation, Astronomy, and
Flight Indoctrination. Both completed the Army's
parachute jump training at Ft Benning and competed
on the Academy's team. The Spartan life suited them
both well, but each knew this was only a trade school
prepping them for their futures. They accepted that
and did very well.

The rigorous schedule of being a cadet coupled with
the physical difficulties of being twenty miles from the
nearest co-ed school had seriously hampered their
dating successes. This had always been one of the
drawbacks of this cadet life. There had been some
strange dates and some stranger women in their lives,
but too many of the locals had marriage on their
minds. Pete wanted to spend some of his immediate
future seeing and sampling the world. He fully
expected to settle down some day, but for now, it was
basically "love 'em and leave 'em". Women loved his
gentle toughness and his natural wit. He was smooth as

eighteen-year-old Scotch and left many broken hearts. He loved women, but not a woman.

Dave, on the other hand, still carried a thing for Dawn and had thought several times about trying to contact her. Her phone number was no longer any good, and the greasy spoon where she had worked had no info on her whereabouts. He figured she had hooked up with her "Charlie" and was off in the Air Force somewhere. He wondered if they would ever again meet and what would happen if they did. Every woman he was with was only a temporary replacement, a euphemism for someone who could have and should have been a fixture within his life. He knew he had to get over this but was in no hurry. Still he kept the unfolded paper with the lipstick smudge in his billfold where she had put it four years earlier.

The freedom, position and privilege of being a Firstie, a senior, was good reward for suffering through the first three years as a cadet and a good transition back into real life. And one of the most cherished benefits was owning a car. Both being car guys, Dave bought a cherry split-window Vette, and Pete, a Goat with 3 twos and four on the floor. Just knowing that they could hop in their car and head for the lights of the city or just hang out at one of the many local neighborhood bars gave a new feeling of freedom and reality. It was a year of transition for those who were wise enough to exercise it. Dave never passed that truck stop without thinking again of Dawn…but he never stopped.

Pete and Dave and their classmates were looking forward to selecting their flight training bases, which would happen somewhere around 100th Night. With their higher class standings, each would probably get their first choices: Randolph Field in San Antonio for Pete and Williams AFB in the Arizona desert for Dave. Pete had never been to Texas and wanted to experience the Wild West. Dave just wanted to stay near the mountains and looked forward to the clear flying weather of the desert. They had been inseparable for the past four years, and this transition from the Academy to the "real Air Force" would bring them to face many new issues. Gone now would be the secure feeling of living under the Honor Code, having someone prepare your food and clean your clothes, and toughest of all, actually having to choose what to wear each day. Gone were summer breaks, spit shines, sleeping in our own bed and having someone else plan your 24-hour schedule. Ah, freedom, damned freedom, the double-edged sword.

Nothing could have prepared them for life beyond the South Gate of the Academy. Two hours after Graduation, each had cleared their room and the Academy paperwork and was ready to head south. Dave and Pete walked together down to the parking lot where their loaded cars awaited and paused. They had been the best of friends and had supported and protected each other for four years. They knew this day was soon to come but neither was prepared for the split. Pete was the first to break the silence.

"You already know this, but I am going to really miss you, buddy."

Dave just stood there…tears welling in his eyes. "This is harder than I expected. But I'm going to say this once and only once. I have never told anybody that I loved them, but I'm telling you now and here. You have meant more to me over these past fours years than you will ever know. You have been my rock. You have always been there for me and always kept me on the right track. I don't know what else to say. I could not have made it through this without you and owe you so much. I'm going to miss the hell out of you…and that's it. It's been a good ride."

Pete put his arms around Dave. "This is only the beginning. We will always be together…even when we're not. This Air Force is too small for them to keep us apart. Let's make a pact. Let's meet here again someday and fish Stanley together. Hell, we might even bring our wives and kids."

Dave smiled. "Your fat old wife and your six kids probably won't be able to make the climb."

"Screw you, plow boy."

Dave put his hand on Pete's cheek, climbed in his Vette and started down the hill. Just before he got out of sight, he flipped his friend a thumbs-up.

This moment was as lonesome as Pete had ever been…bittersweetness spread between the security and fellowship of his Academy stint and the rush of excitement of what lay before him. When he first came to Colorado, he claimed a new life. Now as he prepared to leave it, he realized that these past four years had only been a niche in time to prepare him for his life. But what a niche, and what a life!

Pete stopped his car abeam the airfield just before the South Gate and looked back at Stanley Canyon. How many times had Dave and he hiked up that trail? It was a special time in a special place. Stanley provided a calm in the Academy storm. It was where he went to sharpen his coping tools. It symbolized his love for his comrade, his love for the Academy and his new found self and freedom. This moment must last him the rest of his life.

There was little traffic on I-25 since it was a Wednesday. Pete's Goat loved the open road, and he could feel the growl of his 389 through dual Smitty glass packs. The challenge was to keep it close to the speed limit. One doesn't drive the Colorado highways long without learning about the "bear-in-the-air". He passed a few of his classmates also heading south. Three hours later, he stopped in New Mexico for a bite to eat. He then headed east across the desert toward the Texas panhandle and watched as the Rocky Mountains sank lower toward the horizon and finally disappeared in his rear-view mirror. This part of his young life had come to an end. He would only return to Colorado once more.

* * *

16

Flight School hosts a strange recipe of stress, fear, fellowship, joy and growth. It, like the Academy, is a trade school, built on engineering principle, history, dedication, bravado and pride. And, like the Academy, there is a drive and a plan for ultimate success… chocked full of opportunities for total failure. It is an all-or-nothing scenario. If one completes the program, a career and life of flying awaits. But if one fails, then it all ends…and you are back on the road. There is no in-between and no short cuts. Either you succeed or you fail. There are no half-pilots.

Academy grads seem to adapt well to this new lifestyle, for they experienced much of the same pressures and issues back at The Zoo. Their shortcoming seemed to be their lack of experience in real life issues…getting the bills paid, being on-time, scheduling, some social skills, etc.

By the time they reach Flight School, candidates have already completed a Flight Indoctrination Program to demonstrate their basic aptitude and skill package for flying. They have made it through the first of many passages en route to being a fully accredited and operational military pilot. Pete and Dave were on the track to become combat fighter pilots...first, complete Flight School, and then, on to Advanced Fighter School.

Flight School lasts about one year, first qualifying in a basic jet trainer, and then moving up to the T-38, an advanced twin-engine, super-sonic jet. The candidate's day is generally split between the classroom and the cockpit, with lots of time in the simulator. Classroom subjects include aerodynamics, thermodynamics, weather, engineering, physiology and navigation. The flying portion includes basic flight dynamics, formation, aerobatics, instrument flying, night flying and cross-country. There is little time for distraction. Hangovers and head colds are accepted, but not appreciated. One must be ready to fly every day... mentally, physically and emotionally. Mediocrity is not an acceptable exception. Excellence is both the standard and the minimum. Pilot is not just a noun or a verb. It is a way of life, a journey of learning and wisdom, an attitude of bravado and can-do, a commitment to mission and a dedication to all things good and the American way of life. One learns to live bullet proof with ample opportunities to prove you are not.

Dave and Pete were both good athletes and well coordinated. They were comfortable with wherever they were in space. Both were smart and highly dedicated to becoming the world's greatest fighter pilot. They were cut out for this flying business and performed well in training. Their natural competitiveness had them on the phone quite often together touting how each was better than the other. And they were good...good enough to finish their training at the tops of their class. At Graduation from flight School, each was presented the coveted silver bowl, the Commander's Cup, the symbol of being the top student. As one would expect, Pete earned higher grades in the procedure-laden instrument flying while Dave excelled at formation and aerobatics. Dave was more of a fly-by-the-seat-of-your-pants pilot, and as such, he would on occasion raise the ire of his Instructor Pilot by his lackadaisical attitude toward procedures. Finally, Dave's IP made it clear to him that the Air Force owned the planes, the concrete, the parachute and oxygen mask...everything except his underwear and his big watch. They owned it all... and if Dave wanted to play the game, he'd better play it by the AF rules...or else. Dave got the message and developed into one of the finest pilots to come out of the program. His Squadron Commander even suggested to Dave that he forget fighters and stay on as a T-38 instructor.

Flying came a bit tougher for Pete, but he relied on his motto from his cadet days...if they can do it, so can I. His persistence would once again carry him through in finest fashion. Once he got past a bit of airsickness at the start, he, too, captured honor after honor.

One of the benefits of finishing high in your class at Flight School is that you have a better selection of follow-on assignments...and that alone can be great motivation when there is war brewing. When it was

time for choosing, Air Force offered the top students
at each flight training base the opportunity to join
a newly forming squadron with a new concept of
aircraft. These were light-weight fighters, but with an
interesting high-tech twist. They were designed to fly
with a robotic wingman. It was the latest in the fighter
world and drew in both Dave and Pete and several
others from their Academy class.

The concept was interesting. Every time the fighter
pilot flew, he would have a highly responsive and
programmed robot on his wing. The concept had
been developed initially at Wright-Patterson AFB in
the Advanced Systems Lab, and the airframes were
just beginning to come off the production lines in Ft.
Worth. The fighters and the robots were scheduled
to be arriving at Davis-Monthan AFB in Tuscon soon
after the pilots. The training syllabus called for the first
100 hours of flying to be solo…with no wingman. The
pilots would learn the airplane and the tactics. Then
they would learn the capabilities of the robots and
develop "a personal relationship" with the computer
brains on-board both the robot and the fighter.

Pete and Dave were scheduled to arrive at D-M the
same day to report to their new unit, the "Bots"…
TAC's 21st Fighter Squadron. They were looking
forward to joining up again, telling war stories of flight
school, meeting their new squadron mates and just
hanging out. Life was good…but not easy. Air Force
wanted to expedite this new weapons system into the
looming war on the Korean peninsular, so the pressure
was on. The challenge was to learn to fly the fighter as
well as learning and programming your unique robot

software. It really did not matter which robot airframe
flew your wing…only that it was programmed with
your unique codes. Tactics needed to be developed.
The whole concept needed to be validated while
the aircrews were developing their skills. A two-year
process was to be completed and the squadron in place
in Asia within six months.

Not unlike flight school, pilots' time was split between
the classroom and the cockpit. Getting motivated to
study was much easier for Dave, for now it was the
real deal. They were going to war, with real bullets
and missiles that were significantly faster and more
agile than any plane. In the classroom, they learned
the systems of both airframes, the fighter and the
robot, and how to personally customize the robot's
flight behavior and responses. They understood the
necessity of developing tactics on the fly as this concept
matured. Pete and Dave were good study mates since
they approached this task from opposite poles.

Since the squadron had only two two-seat fighters, each
pilot got three dual flights with an IP…then they were
on their own. Initially, all flights were without robotic
wingmen. Once each pilot had proven his proficiency
in the airplane, had completed all classroom work,
and had completed the initial programming of a
robot, he was cleared to fly with a robot on his wing.
The pair flew aerobatics, formation in trail and in
route, instrument approaches, air-to-air tactics, ground
attack, gunnery range and simulated emergencies.
Each pilot would tweak the robot's software continually
to make it his perfect wingman. Some created a robot
that would think like and react just like them. Others

went to great extremes to create a wingman who would do everything just the opposite. Repetition breeds predictability...and in combat, that can prove to be a fatal flaw. Nevertheless, each pilot was responsible for the ultimate programming of his robot...within military reason. These expert systems were wingmen based on Artificial Intelligence, customized by their pilots to be the perfect assistant.

The final check flight for Pete and Dave, as well as the other 36 pilots, required each pilot to take his robot to one of six remote landing strips, land and refuel his pair. Then when each received clearance, each would take off with their wingman, proceed to a specified gunnery range for a ground assault demo and evaluation, then on to a specified checkpoint and enter into a simulated air-to-air encounter with another robot pilot. Every part of the final check was highly monitored, for this was also the validation of this new concept.

Although the cloak of secrecy was tightly drawn on this entire breakthrough program, it was difficult to disguise a bunch of newly designed airplanes departing Tuscon, each with some smaller aircraft flying in formation. But it was important to keep this weapons system a surprise for the Asian enemy as well as for the Russians.

Because of the rush to get this new weapons system into combat, Dave and Pete were flying twice a day most every day and often on Saturdays. Even after they had passed all check rides and were fully combat qualified, they continued to fly daily, honing their skills and learning their robot wingman's capabilities. By the time their entire Bot Squadron was checked out and ready to go to war, they had each accumulated over 600 hours of flight time. Now they were ready to pack up the entire squadron and head for their Korean base...and combat. Ferry pilots would bring the aircraft by way of Alaska, and C-5s would bring the robots. The pilots would stop en route to complete the jungle survival school in the Philippines.

Neither Dave nor Pete had ever been far outside the States...certainly never to the jungles of the Philippines. They both looked forward to the experience. Dave was especially interested to see the jungle and learn how to survive in it. Both he and Pete had attended the survival program at the Academy... but this was different. This school could determine whether they survived if they ever had to eject from their plane. And even more important, it would teach them about life as a POW in the Asian scenario. Much had been learned from the Viet Nam war as to how prisoners were treated and how to survive the ordeal.

The first week of Jungle Survival School, better known as Snake School, was spent in the class room learning the techniques and tactics, what to avoid and how to prepare foods found in the jungle and in prison camp...like rats and beetles. One must find and digest protein to stay alive and healthy. The second week was spent living in the jungle and on the run...how to escape and evade the enemy. This week was spent moving from one place to another with the instructor, a local native, showing where to find food and how to prepare it. The third and final week was spent in POW camp. On the last leg of the escape and evasion trek, students were told to arrive at a particular checkpoint in the jungle just at sundown. There the students found a large bonfire where their Negrito instructors told them to wait...and then silently disappeared into the jungle.

When the last of the students had arrived at the fire, Asian men dressed in black fatigues and carrying AK-47 assault rifles appeared from the jungle and ordered each of the students to put a cloth sack over their heads. Then one-by-one, each had their hands taped together behind their backs with duct tape. A bamboo pole was stuck between their backs and their arms and again secured with duct tape. Another piece of tape was wrapped around their eyes. Anyone who protested had a bamboo pole shoved up between their legs. The prisoners were forced into a line, and a rope was looped around each neck to keep them in line like a bunch of geese. They were led in this fashion for what could not have been over a hundred meters, and even with the sacks taped over their eyes, the prisoners could tell they were in some sort of a structure. One-by-one, each prisoner was taken out of line and thrown into a prison cell, three-feet square and six feet tall. It was up to the individual prisoner to rid himself of the sack and the pole and the tape...and each did. Immediately the tap code messages began and plans for escape attempts were made. The captors played a loud recording of a baby crying both to harass the prisoners and to block the use of the tap code.

After about an hour, each prisoner was pulled from his cell, strip searched and given only a rat-eaten pair of black pants to wear. The guards took everything else from the prisoners, including any jewelry, their boots and under-garments...everything. After a week in the jungle, most of these pilots' flight suits were already well shredded. Then they wrote their prisoner number across their foreheads with an indelible marker. Any protest was answered with a rifle butt into the stomach or a shock to the groin from a cow prod. Then the prisoner was thrown back into his cell.

Each cell had a gravel floor and concrete walls and ceiling. The only light in the cell was that which came in under the door. In each cell was a honey bucket with a board on top for cover. After the first day of isolation, each of the "students" in this school was beginning to wonder what they had gotten themselves into. The reality of the isolation, the physical harassment of the guards, the hunger and lack of water coupled with the knowledge that you were isolated from any protection thousands of miles from home really began to work on each mind. Each knew this was a school designed to teach them how to stay alive, but the pain and the fear were real. The guards seemed to be enjoying their roles a little too much. Sometime during the second day, Pete found himself talking to the gravel illuminated by the thin strip of light coming in under the door. They seemed to have faces and were moving around. Pete wondered if he were losing his mind.

About twice each day, the guards would come and drag each student from his cell, tape his hands behind him and place a cloth sack back over his head. They would shove him into a too-small wooden crate out in the tropic sun and close a door tightly behind him. Then they would beat the crate with bamboo poles.

After one of these treatments, Dave was dragged from the crate, every muscle cramped, and forced into a small wooden chair. The captors spread his legs and taped them to the legs of the chair. His arms were forced over the back of the chair. When they removed the sack from his head, Dave found himself in a small office before a large desk. The guards left the room, giving Dave a chance to look around and evaluate his situation.

Behind the desk was a large photo of Chairman Mao and some flag with a red star on it. To his right was a mirror, appropriately placed so he could see the miserable situation he was in...filthy, scraped up, half-naked, stripped of his every belonging and taped to a chair...totally helpless. Across the desk lay an electric cow prod...carefully left in clear view to intimidate the prisoner.

From a side door entered a small-framed Asian man in a dark green uniform. He didn't look at Dave, but went straight to his desk and began to study a folder there. "Prisoner 22, would you like a glass of water?"

"Eat shit," Dave fired back. "And my name is Edwards, Lieutenant, born 15 June..."

"Now, now, now," interrupted the interrogator. "Let's not be that way. I already know all about you. Our intelligence is very good. You were born in Montana. You are what you Americans call a cowboy...but then

America is far away now, isn't it, David. Is it alright if I call you David?"

Dave did not answer.

"I do have a few simple questions for you, David. I am wondering why you came so far, all the way from Montana to Asia to kill our peace-loving people here. What could your government have told you about us to make you want to do that?"

Dave still kept silent.

"David, tell me about your airplane. When you were shot down by our brave gunners, we did not recognize what you were flying. Is it something new? Why don't you tell me about it?"

In the classroom, his instructors had taught him that if you continue to stonewall an interrogation, your captors may just kill you. They didn't need any more POWs, for they really had enough for political reasons, and one more prisoner, one way or the other, was only more work for them. Dave needed to practice this skill in this rugged academic situation. He had to have some intercourse with this interrogator to survive.

"Under the Geneva Convention, I can only give you name, rank, serial number and date of birth…and you seem to have all that stuff already."

"Now, David, you don't seem to understand what's going on here. I work for a very mean gentleman who requires me to gather such items of information. If I don't get some information from you, he will not be happy with me…or with you. It is so much easier if you just answer my questions...easier on both of us." His attitude stiffened. "Now tell me about your airplane!"

"Eat shit and die."

The interrogator picked up the cow prod and came around the desk to stand directly before Dave. "You give me few choices, Lieutenant Edwards." He kicked Dave squarely in the chest with his boot, knocking Dave and his chair over backwards. Dave was taped to the chair and totally helpless. The interrogator shoved the prod up Dave's pants and into his groin and pulled the trigger. Dave braced for the pain, but it never happened. "Dave, in a real situation, you would have just experienced the end of your family tree." He winked at Dave. "Guards, get this SOB back in his cell."

Each of the other students at Snake School had experienced similar treatment during multiple interrogations. It had been a tough experience. Some talked. Some didn't. But in the big picture, it had been good training for what was to come. And to the man, each was glad when it was over. This school had made going into combat the easier of two paths.

* * *

17

Dave and Pete sat next to each other on the C-130 ride from the Philippines to their new base at Taegu, Korea. They had a lot to talk about. One of the POW skills they had learned in Snake School was to tell the enemy something without telling them anything. The enemy can always torture you enough to make you say something. The point is to tell them nothing of importance. If they could read it in <u>Aviation Week</u> anyhow, then tell them just to keep them from killing or maiming you.

During one of his interrogations, Pete's interrogator had called Pete non-professional. Pete had countered that he was more of a professional soldier than the interrogator…at which time the interrogator bet Pete he could prove Pete wrong and stuck out his hand to seal the bet. Just as Pete shook his hand, the flashbulbs went off, and the enemy had a picture of Pete "collaborating" with the enemy. It was a tough school but a good one. As in most academic situations, each student could practice a skill safely that could someday save their lives.

After four hours in a C-130, everyone was glad to have the Loadmaster tell them to prepare for landing. The comfort of the nylon troop seats must have been designed to encourage troops to get off the plane and fight somebody. And the closer one gets to landing, the more uncomfortable they become.

Most of their bags and flight equipment had already come over on the C-5s carrying the drones, so each pilot only had a duffle for the essentials. Most of the flight boots and flight suits had become a victim to Snake School and stayed in the PI. The Loadmaster announced that at the request of the Base Flight Surgeon everyone should form a line beneath the wing of the C-130…and drop their pants. They were each welcomed to Korea with a gamma globulin shot that felt like a roll of quarters inserted beneath the skin on the cheeks of their butts.

Taegu was a bit hilly and covered in jungle…not as dense as the Philippines, but with enough layers of canopy to hide the ground from the sun. Much of the jungle had been destroyed during the Korean War of the early 50s, but the jungle always returns. And everything smelled of the earth. It reminded Dave of Boy Scout camp when he was a boy.

The base was old, having originally been built by the UN forces in the previous war. Many of the Aces of that Korean War that Pete and Dave had learned of at the Academy had walked these same dusty streets and hung out at the O-Club bar and played softball at the diamond out by the radar site. But this was not their war…even though they had left theirs unfinished for a new generation to wrap up.

Base facilities were good. The billets were clean and air conditioned…but not spacious. And the mess was blessed with a good cook who loved French Apple Pie and could make great ice cream from powdered milk. Who could ask for more? The only round-eyed woman on base was uglier than home-made soap, but kept the General happy.

It had been almost a month since the pilots of the Bot Squadron had flown. And in that month, the squadron, its planes and its support forces had all moved to Korea. The planes had all arrived safely, and the last few of the robots were almost in commission. Everyone was anxious to get back to flying and to try out the new weapons system.

Flying started with missions sans the robots, giving the pilots time to learn the territory and the new fighters. The first missions included both MiG Cap and some ground attack. Pilots flew missions almost daily for five weeks straight and then stood down for a week. And after the first few weeks, they were combat experienced and ready for their wingmen. It doesn't take long to become a hardened combat pilot, for the realities of war are always close at hand. You either deal with it and learn, or you die…or worse, you contribute to someone else's death. Combat losses become very evident in a close family of combatants. And the loss of the first pilot, a classmate of Pete and Dave, brought home to everyone that this is war and the risks are high and permanent...and very often, personal. The hole left in the lives of the aircrews was irreparable and irreversible. You just learned to deal with it. Death became part of living.

War is hell and it matters little whether you happen to be one of the horrified unfortunates with their boots in the mud or one of the glorified unfortunates hanging on a thread of faith called aerodynamic principle. Death comes quickly and slowly, continuously, always haunting those combatants who raise clenched fist to its grimly lit face, but always and in all ways, it comes. Dying can come in a blinding flash with no warning, pain or consideration, or it can dwell forever in our memory as we share in recall the fate of a fallen comrade or revisit those dark corners of our minds where only the most private horrors reside. But always it comes.

Combat is one of those things that you have to experience for yourself. If someone asked you to tell them about being in combat, they wouldn't have a prayer of truly understanding. The words and descriptions just cannot fully describe the terror... and the thrill. How do you describe the feeling of tracers passing so close to your aircraft that you can smell them...knowing that the next one might be the Silver BB with your name on it? How do you describe the sound and the feeling of rounds passing through your fuselage, sounding like someone straightening a bent car fender with a ball peen hammer? How do you describe flying over that burned spot on the side of the mountain where your buddy crashed and burned and died just days before? How do you describe the sorrow of packing up that last foot locker of his stuff to send to the grieving family, fully knowing that he won't be the last to go the same way? And for what? If you survive, you go home to those who hate you and spit on you and call you "killer". You spend the rest of your life with a mind and heart full of shadows and memories that might resurface at any moment for you to relive the horrors one more time after time after time.

Yet to many, combat flying is a competition...you against the enemy, the politicians, the odds, the elements and fate. And the thrill of the competition must be factored in, for many choose to return to combat to relive the thrill. In combat, the soldier is part of an enormous machine on a mission, with good chances of success and victory. Flying in combat is the greatest thrill of them all...flying a wonderful air machine equipped with all the power, technology and destructive elements that you can get off the runway and into the air. This is flying at its finest, with few restrictions and unlimited glory.

General Patton told the story of the returning Roman conqueror as he re-entered Rome preceded by his captured booty...the slaves, the gold and treasure, the animals. Yet as he prepared to accept the accolades of his leaders, the slave standing behind him in his golden chariot whispered in his ear..."All glory is fleeting." And thus it is the way of the glory-seeking combat pilot. Today's glory has a short half-life and must always be replenished...day after day...mission after mission. It becomes an addiction. And so is born the war-lover.

Dave and Pete were more alike than different. But perhaps the greatest difference between them was their individual definition of competition. Dave had always been competitive. He wanted to win...period. And he did most of the time. He was always up to a challenge of any hue and expected to win. He would challenge anyone, any time, without fear...and simply would not accept loss. Victory was his game and his focus... even when it came to his best friend, Pete. On the other hand, Pete's view of competition had changed in his maturation. He had come a long way from the Philadelphia streets where winning was everything. His greatest challenge now came from within. He was his own best competition. He understood and accepted his personal skill levels and strived constantly to carry himself to higher and higher levels. He was his own competition. His measure of doing well was when he knew he had done his best. Hence, he could accept losing, if he had done his best...but never losers. Likewise, he found winning distasteful if he knew he had not performed at his best. If there were any reward in achievement for Pete, it was gathered in the journey of effort, not in the destination goal of success.

The difference between the two is that Dave's philosophy always created winners and losers... and Dave had no problem with that as long as he was the winner. Those were simply his expectations, and he made no excuses for the way he felt. On the other hand, Pete's approach only created losers, for Pete judged himself only against himself, and perfection, the best he could do, always became the new minimum. Victory was short lived and rarely appreciated. This philosophy created a high achiever in Pete, but one who seldom celebrated his numerous victories.

And so it was in combat. While Washington and the newspapers want to make combat a numbers game with body counts, both US and enemy, trucks destroyed, missions flown, tonnage delivered, etc, the soldier views it differently…mostly as a game of survival. Every risk must be balanced against the pay-off. The stakes are high. The results of the competition are permanent…and normally deadly for some contender.

So in the grand scheme, all is placed in this balance of life…the fear and horror versus the glory and thrill. Every situation and every combatant is different. Some are drawn to it like a tongue looking for the missing tooth, and others wisely run away from it. And one never knows which he is until he has experienced it for himself. But if you choose to stay and play, you push all the chips to the table. It's a win-or-lose game, and winners often go looking anxiously for the next chance to play.

* * *

18

With seven months now in theater, Pete was well experienced and somewhat hardened to the realities of his having the grim reaper always at six o'clock low, the result of living in a combat squadron where eight of the 38 pilots had already lived in fame and gone down in flame, now just a number, no longer a name. His house was in order, and if the fates pointed that crooked finger his way, he would meet that challenge just as he had done xxxx143 times before, for whatever the risks were that lay before him and he knew them all, it was worth it just to be a combat pilot, just to raise his fist, just to meet the ultimate challenge, just to push it all to the line. Live fast, love them all and die young. And indeed he should have died some four times already in this last of his 25 years.

The bad guys needed to continually resupply their troops, and since the water was under total control of the US Navy, they were limited to land and air. Radar picked up heavy air traffic coming down from the north almost every night. The radar Doppler signature identified them as rotary wing, but the question was always the same. Who were they? Too often, we didn't know if they were the enemy or perhaps, Air America or Continental Air Service. They were out there doing what they do and never coordinated with the Air Force. A visual identification was necessary to ensure it was the enemy. Their terrain following flight patterns and low airspeeds kept them safe from conventional fighters. Heat seeking missiles would have been the weapon of choice, except for the cost of the missile, the limited supply and the ID issue. Some cost effective method was needed to counter these choppers, and the task fell on the Bot Squadron. Ground radar would vector the fighter/robot combo into the area so the fighter would not need to expose himself to enemy radar. The fighter would identify the chopper through its IR signature, verify the target to the robot and release him to engage the chopper. Undetected, the robot would approach the target from the rear and one hundred feet above, matching the flight velocity and path of the chopper. The robot carried a canister under its wing containing light cable on a reel and would unwind the cable, flying it into the chopper's rotor system. The cable would break loose from the robot at the canister, entangling the rotor and the flight controls, bringing down the chopper. After two weeks of having their choppers mysteriously disappear, the enemy flights stopped.

Resupply by truck was an entirely different issue, with its own special requirements and threats. The loaded Commie trucks would travel south by night and stay concealed under the jungle canopy during the day. These truck parks were generally heavily defended by AAA and missile sites. Therefore, it was safer to attack

them at night when they were on the move. These
were typical ground assault missions for the squadron
and were much more exciting than taking down the
choppers. But enough of the trucks got through to
make this a continuing mission...every night. And that
was Pete's mission for this night.

There is never "just another mission", for each brings
its own set of circumstances and players. The pieces,
though somewhat the same, never are and never quite
fit into the same pattern, with some pieces missing and
some from another war or another world. For this Pete
was thankful, for warfare becomes boring and death
mundane when the outcome is as predictable and
missions, like his comrades, become numbers without
names.

Was this mission to be different even though it was
the same as so many of his other search-and-destroy
sorties? Pete knew the real estate along this stretch of
jungle trail as well as he knew the beer joints along
Academy Boulevard. After all, he had spent a lifetime
these past few months looking down into this jungle
rainforest, searching for luckless targets of opportunity
and hoping that in the final tally, he would kill more
enemy trucks than monkeys and banana trees. Was
this feeling deep in the pit of his stomach indicative of
what was to come or just the remnants of last night's
malaria tablet washed down with a liter of Singha beer?
It mattered little to Pete as he parked his bike outside
the tactical operations center, for he was terminally
afflicted with that numbness that insidiously eats at
the moral fiber of the professional trained killer that
he had become. The razor edge polished by months

of training had dulled and rusted in the muck of intentional human destruction of human...all in freedom's name.

Pete was really no different from the hundreds of thousands of the green-clad cogs in the war machine, nor was he different from the tens of thousands who would return home under draped flag. He was almost past the point of caring, having been there long enough to see through the facade of glories promised and yet too distant from the venture's end. Because of the limited number of robot pilots, they were not eligible for the 100-mission early out and were flying well past the recommended 75-hour per month limit. Most of the surviving original robot pilots were simply worn out and burned out.

Several hours of today's yesterdays had been spent in the time-honored tradition of mission-planning, now somewhat a lost art. Pilots, and Ops officers, and mechanics, and even the highest levels of the DOD, the source of all wisdom and directives, had succumbed to allowing the smart computers to compose all original thinking, now another lost art. These experts-on-a-chip supposedly combined all human knowledge and history, from the latest G-2 intelligence to childhood deprivations of the enemy commander. Even George Patton, the finest example of military historian, could not have imagined a more complete study or evaluation of the situation. Indeed, every possible contingency had been considered. Nothing could possibly go wrong. Nothing.

Into the computers had been placed every piece of the puzzle plus a few extras that some of the Pentagon think-tank tinkers had thought necessary to maintain control on an unruly set of military commanders. After all, all command and clever thought must reside inside the Beltway. Where better to learn of warfare and tactics than in the jungles of the Ivy League? And the real war is only a phone call or a Life magazine away. Pre-WWII Japan dwelled in the ROM and the fear of losing control, influence and bureaucratic position to a bunch of unenlightened Academy and trade school mercenaries was unthinkable...even heresy. What is good for American business and American politics is so obviously good for American youth.

Yet, Pete had learned in his short combat career that the gook with the Commie rifle could give a hoot-in-hell about expert systems and that the only chip a gook would ever see would be in the Seiko watch he takes from the battered body of the downed Yankee Air Pirate. Pete took his time with his mission planning, just as if his life and his obtrusive watch depended upon it. All of the latest intel had been entered from last night's missions, as were the other sorties planned for his sector during his flight. Rules of thumb and trends, history and statistics, other pilot inputs and the fictitious Rules of Engagement all were there. Unfortunately, these facts had been jaundiced by rules created within the hallowed walls of ivy but the clever combat pilot could weave through even these. Pilots were no longer just jet jockeys and trash haulers. They, of survival necessity, had become knowledge engineers and programmers.

The mission for this day was as before, multi-ship search and destroy, along the "Valley Highway", a hundred miles of bad road for both the gunner and the runner. The myriad of trails used for resupply of the war in the southern provinces funneled into one super-trail of mud holes, bomb craters, optically and radar-guided AAA, small arms, missiles, logistic dumps, and even a couple of HoJos that were generally avoided, for even the enemy grunt deserves a hot meal every once in a while. The surrounding mountains forced the merging of the many trails and presented quite a problem to the runner, the poor bastard who risked his life and his sack of rice driving hand-me-down Commie duece-and-a-halfs up and down this stretch. But equally as endangered was the gunner, who although was flying good machinery against lucrative targets, faced more flak than did Bill Holden at To-Kori. They had to keep this cow path open at all costs, and the costs were high. Pete had to keep it closed and his costs were higher.

The computer commanded a 0500 launch to put the time-over-target just before sun-up when the last trucks would just be approaching their truck park. The element of surprise weighed highly in the mission planner, a concern of Pete, for how many times does the enemy get hit at sun-up before the element of surprise is no surprise at all? How much feed-back does the computer have to get that the enemy is ready for this tactic before it discards this heuristic? He had already noticed that the AAA was more and the targets were fewer on these early morning milk runs. He hoped the computer was paying attention, but then what did the damned computers with their ivy-league flunkies care about gooks and mud holes and the invisible enemy in a war that doesn't exist here in a neutral country?

The early morning briefing held few surprises, just an intel update downloaded from aircraft still en route back from Pete's operating area, plus assignment of crews and tail numbers. The dolt in the starched fatigues that posed as the Intel officer simply read from the greenline frag just received by "Big Brother", the end-of-the-line terminal from HQ. Pete was certain the enemy had a similar terminal and were being briefed at the same time about his upcoming mission. The latest code words were being issued and Safe Areas for bail out reviewed. Radio freqs, armament loads, no questions. 0500 launch.

Pete recalled how some things never change as he took a nervous pee at the survival equipment hooch. He was willing to bet his mission whiskey that David had pissed in the creek that ran down to the Philistine camp as he picked out the stones for Goliath's brow. A slingshot of another era, his Smith and Wesson Combat Masterpiece, Pete carefully loaded with the shiny brass jackets that cradled the homemade and unauthorized dum-dum slugs, another violation of the infamous, and oft violated, Rules of Engagement, but he hoped to kill all potential complaints in his own way. Strapped around his waist beneath his flight suit in an area where gook custom made them embarrassed to search, his money-belt hid his plastic escape and evasion map, water purification tablets, diet pills to keep him awake if he was forced to escape and evade, a couple of small devices to let gook blood, and a three-day compass. He intended to walk home if the gook gunners got lucky. Be prepared. In the heel of each boot was a wire finger saw, with another slipped into the waistband of his flight suit along with some snare wire, a couple of rubbers for water storage and another three-day compass. It was called a three-day compass, for if you were about to be captured, you swallowed it…and three days later when it again appeared, you swallowed it again.

The green fuzzy stuff growing on the leather holster sewn onto his mesh survival vest reminded him of just how long he had been exiled to this swamp. It did not bother him that he actually talked to the stuff and called it by name, for he figured it was living near this swamp long before his arrival and would survive long after his demise. There is something immortal about green stuff in that you cannot beat it and most likely we will someday all join it. This oriental Cudsu grew on dinosaur dung and will survive nuclear radiation. It was blessed with no intelligence.

Pete slipped on his survival vest, checked his extra battery for his survival radio, counted his extra .38 rounds and located the rat shot rounds in case of snake encounter. He slipped his Philippino bolo knife from Snake School down into the sheath between his shoulder blades, insuring that the tip was protected by metal plates just in case he was forced to bail out. The locals shaped them from old Jeep springs, and with it, you could quickly cut a cow path through the jungle undergrowth. And for luck, he swigged from the Chevis he kept in his water bottle. It was not that strong, but it helped mask the flavor of the iodine used to kill the little gremlins that lived in the local water supply. Now let the games begin. He pulled his chute from the peg and his brain bucket. Number 317 was again ready to play war.

* * *

19

The maintenance computer had assigned him aircraft #6400, not only because it was mechanically ready and capable of delivering the dictated ordinance, but also because Pete had been flying it regularly recently and without write-up. Pete appreciated this policy, for it allowed him to become familiar with the old girl and her idiosyncrasies. The pilots had learned that the only way to beat this system and to exit the loop was to write up a couple of mechanical problems, and very soon they would be flying another aircraft. Even if she were showing the scars of heavy combat nearing the end of her first year of life, Pete loved to fly 6400, for she had the best of the wrench-benders for a keeper and had been updated with the latest avionics and support systems. The mechs had given her the handle of "Patches", for reasons Pete was trying to forget.

It really did not matter which of the robotic vehicles was to fly on his wing today, for they were all pretty much the same. These flying pawns were fully programmable, and Pete had developed the piloting software to where he was comfortable with it. Pete

considered the RVs as expendable and as long as
he had a copy of the software secured safely at Ops,
he worried little about his robotic shadow. Having a
robotic wingman and a robotic copilot had worked
to his advantage many times. On two separate sorties
when Pete's on-board computer brain determined it
could neither jam nor outperform Commie SAMs,
it ordered the wingman into position to take the
hit. Pete was thankful that the computers could only
reason and not think.

As he passed through Operations, he signed for his
morphine syringe and the computer CD, the little
compact disc that contained everything anyone could
ever possibly want to know about the mission, the
world, life on other planets and how to win at Keno.
He was always amazed at how his aircraft computer
could read, reason and regurgitate so much info,
the three Rs. The combined intelligence of many
experts, pilots, tacticians, engineers, mechs et al had
been converted into computerese and hidden on this
little plastic disc. Pete was amazed all right, but not
convinced that all correct answers came only from the
computer. If the computer were so damned smart,
why didn't they just let it fly the mission and he would
go play bumper pool in the O-Club bar? Pete felt no
concern that he might get replaced; he felt concerned
that he might not.

During Pete's pre-flight inspections of Patches and
his robotic wingman, which Pete traditionally and
cleverly named "Ming the Merciless" from his Flash
Gordon days as a kid, the mech loaded the CD into
the on-board computer system. Pete liked to use the

call sign "Ming" for his wingman, for it rhymed with wing, was easy to recall during high stress situations, and the computer found it an easy word to recognize in Pete's South Philly accent. The pilots experimented with the voice function of the computer until pilot and computer agreed on a vocabulary. The last thing a combat pilot wants during stress is for the computer to ask "huh?" Likewise, Pete called his on-board computer "R2", short for R2D2, which was not short enough for even Luke Skywalker. The saga continues.

R2 had already knocked up Ming on their secure digital data link, loading him with mission particulars such as pilot intent and how to return to home base should Pete and R2 go down. To protect itself from disinformation, Ming would respond only to Pete's voice pattern through R2's digital input pattern. In the event of Pete's being disabled or a break in the data link, Ming would return to base and initiate the infra-red Instrument Landing System [ILS] approach, evading the enemy threat and downloading its situation awareness intel to the Ops Center computer for rescue purposes. Pete had programmed R2 to have the same capability. This was standard operating procedure across the squadron. Even if everything went bad, something was coming home to tell the story.

Ming's robotic airframe could greatly outperform Patches, for it carried no pilot or life support systems. It could sustain 20g maneuvers yet emulate similar radar and IR signatures as Patches in order to decoy and combat smart surface-to-air missiles. Ming had duplicated R2's computer capability and would come to R2's aid in the case of overload, garbage collecting or partial systems failure. Ming, like R2, was capable of wide-band jamming, and the 3-D picture they composed while terrain following in combat route formation from the combined digital radars allowed supersonic penetrations at 50 feet. Whether in terrain following mode, air-to-air, or ground attack, having Ming's radar watching and communicating with R2 (and vice versa) gave a 3-D God's eye view that Moscow and their North Korean pawns had yet to duplicate or defeat.

The big bombers had again gained a new life using this concept. With their radar images like the rising sun, the B-52s had begun using this technique for their low altitude penetrations. Once launched from the mother ship in a manner similar to their cruise missiles, their tiny robotic wingman, virtually invisible to radar, would fly at 2000 feet above the ground and one mile abeam to the bomber's starboard side. The radar from the wingman was directed toward the area in front of the bomber and the bomber's radar was set at low power with only vertical emissions for radar altitude readout. The secure laser digital communications link was similar to that between Ming and R2 and gave the bomber the wingman's point of view. This penetration technique coupled with a detailed digital map gave new life to the old bombers. It was not as good as current stealth concepts, but it had made the big B-52 bombers a credible weapon for another decade, another war...another 40 or 50 years.

Pete had both aircraft running, and R2 and Ming were checking aircraft systems status when an intel update came in from another aircraft taxiing in from another mission in the same area. Weather was generally good with a few morning cirrus clouds. The enemy radar was the same as briefed with the addition of a Fire Can radar, which is normally associated with a 57mm gun. That meant possible trouble. Its location was noted on R2's digital map and spatial data base. Tactics advisor expert system was notified. Two UHF frequencies were being actively jammed so the communications expert system switched to backups and notified Ming.

Systems checkout came back green, and Pete received clearance to taxi to the runup area. Although Ming was programmed to taxi independently, it had become squadron procedure for wing to taxi first, followed closely by lead. Computer vision worked well in laboratory conditions, but out here in the swamp and the monsoons and the heat and the blowing dust where everything is painted in various shades of olive drab, experience overruled technology. Pete would verbally guide Ming into position. Takeoff was not a problem, for the IR emitters along each side of the runway installed for the IR/ILS kept Ming right on centerline.

Both aircraft survived the Last Chance inspection, guns were hot, and tower had cleared the two-ship for take-off. Pete talked Ming onto the runway centerline and when Ming was confident that it was seeing the proper IR and video picture, it passed through R2 that it was ready to go. Pete took off first, for he did not want Ming airborne without him, in case his aircraft needed to abort during takeoff. Twelve seconds after brake release, R2, sensing no malfunctions of either aircraft, commanded Ming's takeoff.

At 500 feet, Ming was programmed to enter a 30-degree bank right turn to heading 090, to continue climbing at 300 knots at 1000 feet per minute. Pete performed a 360-degree right turn and joined to the inside wing. Once Ming was confident that it recognized Pete, it moved back into wing position and employed R2's systems readout and Patches' IR image to stay there.

The first item in R2's program was to verify the security of the data link with Ming and with the Ops Center computer at Home Plate. By now, the Russian advisors were highly active in seeking out the weaknesses in both the robotic wingman concept and the new laser data link. Allied involvement in the "territorial dispute" required our showing the world, and especially the Russians, the absolute latest in the arsenal of the free world. We, like the Commies, were becoming expert in the field of disinformation, the fine art of leaking the right information to gain the proper effect, whether or not that information were correct. The trick becomes making the receiver a believer.

With a robot on your wing and with the vast amounts of data concerning the mission being returned in real time to the Ops Center computer, the last thing that Pete could afford was to have a spook on his party line. The Commie advisors did some jamming at appropriate times, but jamming could be defeated by the auto-switching function of the communicator expert system. The greater threat was having bogus info that appeared to be the real thing, and the enemy was getting too close. Thus far, the Home Plate hackers, an innovative group of scope dopes with ingenious security schemes, had been able to stay one step ahead of the gook gurus. To them it was a game; to Pete, something more was at stake.

This constant flow of intel back to the Ops Center kept Big Brother in the loop, and sometimes Pete gained comfort in knowing that someone knew at every instant where he was and what his sensors, R2 and Ming were passing. If he varied any from his mission plan, Ops would know it real time, a good situation should he go down but a bad one should he decide to go cruising. He had learned to make the system work to his advantage, how to live and fly under this constant surveillance, and how to cause the data link to go down so mysteriously when he wanted to stray from the strict obedience to his beloved Rules of Engagement...perhaps fly under a bridge or buzz a Russian trawler. Pete was no software guru, but he could pull a circuit breaker with the best of them.

The data link to Ops relayed all bus activity through the Home Plate hackers and on to the battle staff back at base. Big Brother knew how the war was going from their easy chairs in the Command Post and all too often forgot that the war was being fought out in the field, not in the air- conditioned comfort accompanied by Safeway music. Pete could not recall losing even one KIA assigned to that hardship, even though he himself had threatened to shove a flare pistol up the butt of the Ops puke that ordered him to do a couple of slow

low-altitude fly-bys of a crash site in bad guy territory. The SOB even wanted pictures.

Yet the data link allowed Big Brother to react quickly to the situation, and Pete did appreciate that. On one mission, Pete was a bit slow coming off the trigger and sent a few hundred rounds "accidentally" into a gook village, a travesty of the Rules of Engagement that the pilots could usually slip by Big Brother. However, this time it paid off, for the hooch in his gun sight went off like St. Helens. Ops was able to redirect an outbound flight en route to another target into his battle to help clean up this newly discovered supply depot. Sometimes you just get lucky, and Pete always had preferred luck over skill.

Pete's aircraft and the robot were inundated with sensors, both to sample the war through IR and RF returns, and to continually check on the states of the aircraft and the pilot. Many man-years of experience had been stuffed into the memories of R2 and Ming relative to the various systems. If some unexpected combination of systems sensor return arose, R2 and Ming would initiate self-tests, examine pilot intent and the situation, pilot physiological state and the enormous data base to determine possibilities and contingencies. Pete would receive recommended action but would have the last say toward the proper reaction.

Pete had given up the authority to R2 to make certain decisions and to perform reactions to some situations, for he knew that in these instances, R2 could react much quicker and that only R2's speed could protect them. For example, R2 knew the enemy SAM capability better than even the enemy, for R2 and his chip-mates had examined the SAM flight profiles many times and had stored and shared that info. Only they were fast enough to examine in real time the effect of evasion and jamming, predict the outcome, and take the proper reaction. Pete had given R2 the authority to eject him 2 seconds before impact if R2 were 98% certain of a shoot down. It was with great reluctance that Pete had given up this authority, for it just is not a natural instinct for pilots to leave their bird and especially to allow someone else or something else to make that decision for them.

Many times he had wondered if the gook gurus were smart enough to create such a disinformation signal to force the various R2's in the war to bail out their pilots. He recalled the bar talk of how an unknown voice with perfect American English had screamed over the common UHF Guard channel, "Lead, you're on fire. Bail out. Bail out." Two pilots, probably Navy, bailed out of perfectly good airplanes. Both sides of this little war played excellent mind games. and the Petes were the pawns.

In a like manner, our bombers carried a signal generator that triggered the proximity fuses on some of the older models of SAMs that caused their warheads to explode as soon as they came off of safe, which was just after booster burn-out. The rumor around Pete's squadron was that the Allies had developed a means of taking control of the beam-riding missiles and could fly them into their own tracking radars. It sounded all too good to him, for he had been on the receiving end of too many of those telephone poles and he had learned to fear them more than any other of the enemy's tools.

En route to the target area, Ming and R2 monitored and received updates from two other robot flights from their squadron working along the same targeted road segment. The bus data directed from these two flights back to Ops could be deciphered by R2 and contained the most current intelligence Pete could desire. The weather now was a higher overcast than forecasted with a few showers in the area. Enemy radar was active, and R2 filed the location and emitter profile. R2 set up for jamming and recommended to Pete that he change his inbound route of flight to avoid the new enemy threat. Upon Pete's approval, R2 and the mission planner expert system developed a new set of en route tactics, briefed Pete and notified Ops.

Like most other pilots, Pete disliked major changes to his preflighted mission plans. He had lived with the old plan on his mind since yesterday's mission planning and had grown quite familiar with it. From here on throughout the mission, he felt as if he were playing catch-up. R2 not only sensed the anxiety through the physiological monitors, heart and respiratory rates, skin conductance, blood pressure and eye motion, but also expected it from the knowledge engineering that had created his unique programming. R2 was not Pete's creation, nor was it his clone. Pete had customized and personalized R2 to improve the communications and to fine tune R2's ability to help Pete accomplish the mission. R2 held in its memories the rules of thumb, the methods, the tactics and the experience of over two hundred pilots, interviewed extensively by the knowledge engineers and programmers who were his creators. And although R2 was no more than a couple of hundred dollars worth of integrated circuits, the Artificial Intelligence eased Pete's tasks and gave him that comfort and confidence factor as if he were accompanied and advised by those many experts.

Nevertheless, Pete did not like changes, yet he knew they were required. In an effort to ease Pete's concern, R2 gave him a mission update in the format Pete desired. From the spatial data base derived from previous missions and updated by 3-D satellite digital imagery received while en route, R2 presented both God's-eye and pilot's views of the run up the Valley Highway in accelerated time. Pete slowed down the presentation and then re-ran the mission scenario in the area of the new AAA reported near the s-turn south of Tchepone. This was going to be a hot area today, and the new mission plan required his approach from the north rather than out of the early morning sun as he preferred. R2 reminded him that a pull-up off the target into the sun might give him some added protection from the optically and IR guided return fire. Pete agreed with the 43% of the experts residing within R2 who would have planned the mission with the approach from the north initially.

Suddenly, loud warnings sounded through R2 that a ground radar had locked on and a missile was being launched with a high probability of its being directed at Pete. The enemy used a procedure where individual missile site radars were not allowed to emit until just before launch, thus preventing anti-radiation missiles to be used against them. Instead, the large, area surveillance radars located far to the north would track targets and call up only applicable sites for launch. The large radars were capable of random frequency shift for their own protection and were highly defended.

This was one of the few instances where R2 was allowed to react without Pete's approval. It knew already from its intel data base the highest probability of missile type. When the guidance radar turned on, R2 then verified missile type and initiated jamming. IR sensors located the launch site from the change in IR background pattern due to the booster engine exhaust and verified launch with the addition of the reception of the missile proximity fuse and tracking radar. The launch site location was transmitted simultaneously to Big Brother. With six seconds left until impact, Ming was commanded into a position between R2 and the missile, not only to confuse the missile tracking system, but also to take the hit if necessary. Their planned tactic was to present one image to the missile and then break away from each other with two seconds before impact. Experience had shown Pete that the missile could not react quickly enough to choose between the two targets. Additionally, jamming and flares were saved until four seconds before impact to provide the missile guidance a high confidence level falsely and then reduce it to low values again with no time to react. It was a game of seconds and inches. He who blinks is lost.

As preplanned and programmed for this scenario, Ming launched an anti-radiation missile once it had locked the location of the ground radar into memory. Once the gook missile had missed its target or had exploded, the ground radar would cease emitting, but with the location already in memory and a good IR picture of the site, Ming's missile had a very good probability of finding its target. It tracked on the ground radar emission only as long as the emission source agreed with the IR picture. In this manner, if the enemy attempted to draw the missile away by using an alternate false site of emission, the missile would not be fooled.

R2 successfully defeated the oncoming missile when it finally determined and matched the frequency shift pattern of the proximity detector and convinced the missile that it was close enough to explode. And explode it did, some 1200 feet below the flight, a spectacular explosion matching in grandeur the rising sun at the eastern horizon.

The danger inherent in causing the warhead to ignite is that you might be caught in the shrapnel pattern anyhow. But it was a better tactic than the last moment break away, for the enemy was wise to the maneuver and would fire two missiles in tandem. The first one might be defeated, but you were left committed and exposed to the second one.

The aircraft systems expert system was previously alerted to the increase in threat and potential battle damage by the situation assessment expert system when the missile was initially detected. Aircraft sensors were set into auto built-in-test mode when the overpressure and the IR picture of the missile detonation were received. The expert system analyzed simultaneous systems failures much quicker than any pilot, took appropriate action and notified the pilot and Ops. It was capable of sampling the airflow in the boundary layer and listening for changes in the audible noise level, both indicators of battle damage. Its sensitive accelerometers and strain gauges searched for signs of impact and for changes in airframe vibration patterns. The systems data base held the Dash 1 and Dash 2 engineering knowledge information as interpreted by the best systems and aero engineers plus the knowledge and experience of both factory and flight line mechanics. The system was so good that it was standard procedure to use this expert advice in the daily care and feeding of these airframes back at the home drome. All signs were that Patches and Ming escaped undented and undaunted. The only changes noted were, as expected, Pete's vital signs.

* * *

20

The Valley Highway was lush real estate before the
bombing started and would be again soon after the
bombing. That is just how jungle is. The heavy jungle
canopy covered a myriad of sins for the enemy, a
hidden world shielded from the prying eyes of the
Yankee Air Pirates where the trucks resupplying
the war effort could travel at will. The Allies had
developed special weapons and tactics to combat this
effort. Electronic sensors dropped from aircraft were
scattered along the trail to determine the direction
of travel and locations of truck parks. Some were
hung in the trees that could sense the noise in the
jungle below and could read the ignition patterns of
the trucks passing. From this information, the Allies
could determine what kind of truck, its load and
direction. Some sensors were planted in the ground
and read seismic vibration of the trail traffic. All of
this information was captured by drones overhead and
relayed to the Ops computer back at Home Plate. The
Ops computer crunched these bits of information,
applied the heuristics gained from two years of chasing

trucks and provided aircrew like Pete target areas of high probability.

Pete's mission for the day was to try to catch traffic still on the open road at sun-up and, if there were none, to allow R2 and the Ops computer to generate targets. No traffic was visible...only columns of smoke rising from the late night successes from the earlier strikes and numerous craters.

Bombing the high priority targets was a bit boring because the shots are truly in the dark, for the pilots could seldom see the targets and the computer directed the attack. Such was the case when Pete requested targets from R2, who then brought up in order targets one through five on the digital map. Target two was the closest and on Pete's request, R2 gave him a 3-D briefing from intel and satellite imagery. R2 recommended an attack from south to north with a roll-in at 7500 feet and a left turning pull-out due to the rapidly rising terrain to the east. The nearest Safe Area for bailout was heading 090 at seven miles. Pete agreed with R2's selection of tactics and weapons.

Standard procedure, a habit one normally must be careful to avoid in combat, was for Ming to make the first pass cold on these unseen targets to sample enemy reaction and to take a close-up IR peek through the jungle canopy. Ming came up empty on both accounts, so Pete rolled in hot, again with no results. On Ming's second run, their luck improved, but only briefly. The enemy often leaves you alone if your bombs do no damage in hopes that you will mark them off as a target and go on down the road. But Ming's bombs got a secondary explosion so Pete knew something and somebody were under there, and the enemy knew that he knew.

As Ming pulled off the target and broke left, quad ZPU tracer fire followed him up, reminding Pete of a water hose as the stream of fire snaked up into the early morning haze. Pete rolled in to put his bombs close to Ming's and the secondaries. The tracers were quiet on the roll-in, but in the left break, they were waiting for him. It felt like someone sitting on the fuselage behind the cockpit hitting the airplane with a two-pound ballpeen hammer. R2 immediately ran through the systems check and reported a probability of twelve hits in the right wing and aft fuselage. Fuel leakage was significant but no fire. The flight control system was erratic as the secondary hydraulic system was hit in the accumulator and would fail in R2's opinion in about two minutes. R2 had been slightly damaged, but Ming had picked up its functions. Ops had been notified.

Pete was upset at himself about that last break, for he had often feared that he was relying on the computer R2 entirely too much. He would have never gotten into such a predictable pattern on his own. A good soldier must never appear predictable to his enemy. He knew that if the first three passes were identical, then the dumbest of the gook gunners could figure what was going to happen next, and it did. Pete turned for home, disgusted with himself, with a lesson relearned that he needed to tell the other squadron pilots.

The instrument panel in Pete's cockpit was now
beginning to light up with yellow caution lights
and red failure lights. The secondary accumulator
ruptured, filling the cockpit with a hot brown oily
mist coming out of the air vents that coated the
inside of the canopy and Pete's helmet visor, blinding
Pete to any outside reference or view of the artificial
horizon. His every instinct told him he was in a hard
right descending turn. Pete jettisoned the canopy to
clear the cockpit so he could see the instruments and
the outside horizon. As best as he could tell, he was
at about two thousand feet, inverted with the nose
pointed down at about 45 degrees. R2 began "Bail out.
Bail out. Bail out." Pete couldn't save this one, raised
the armrest which concealed the ejection triggers and
squeezed them.

The ejection seat fired just as ordered, carrying Pete
clear of the aircraft. The butt-snapper separated Pete
from the seat, and the zero-delay lanyard initiated an
immediate opening of the parachute. Pete got a good
opening of the chute just before his body crashed
through the top canopy of the jungle. He came to
an abrupt stop when the parachute canopy snagged
the tree limbs, leaving him dangling uninjured some
50 feet in the air and in clear view of anyone on the
ground below.

#6400 had crashed with a huge fireball about a quarter
of a mile north of his position. Since his ejection
came so shortly before the crash, Pete figured that
those on the ground would figure that he went in with
the airplane. Then he realized that those in the air
would probably think the same and wouldn't come

looking for him. He had to get a radio call off to get
the rescue choppers started his way. Normally, a good
ejection with a good chute will automatically set off his
Emergency Locator Transmitter, the beeper, but he
couldn't be sure. He pulled out his emergency radio
from his survival vest and turned on its beeper. Now
they would know he was alive and his location…but so
would the enemy, for they monitored Guard Channel
and would also hear his transmission. Now it was only
a matter of who would get there first. Three minutes
earlier, he was a bullet-proof Steve Canyon in his
invincible air machine. Now he was in deep kimchi.
It's never wise to bail out right over the people
you have just bombed. It tends to really piss them
off.

Pete wasn't feeling much like a super-hero right now.
The good news was that as best as he could tell, he
was not injured…and that was a miracle considering
his low altitude ejection and his crashing through the
jungle canopy. "Good job, asshole. You just crashed a
six million dollar plane and you're hanging in a tree
in Korea with bad guys all around. So what's your next
move? And why am I talking to myself?" He could feel
all the training and experience kicking in. He knew
he had to get down out of this damned tree that had
probably just saved his life and get away from the
crash site. He connected one end of his tree let-down
device to his parachute harness and the other end to
the risers just above the quick disconnects. He had
never tried this before, but knew how it was supposed
to let him down to the ground. He took a deep
breath and tugged open the quick disconnects, which

disconnected him from his parachute. Then
the plan was to control his descent downward as the
line unreeled through the clamp in his hand. He
had forgotten just how much line was available and
hoped he got to the ground before it ran out...and he
just did.

Pete quickly got out of his remaining parachute
harness and dumped his helmet, water wings and
G-suit. He thought about hiding them, but what
difference would it make? That empty parachute was
clue enough for the enemy to know he was out of the
airplane and alive and on the run...if and when they
found it. He headed directly away from the burning
airplane as fast as he could through the dense jungle,
hacking away the vines with his bolo knife. He couldn't
make good time due to the underbrush, but figured
neither could anyone pursuing him. He just had to
keep moving and not stumble into anyone. He thought
back to his Snake School experience and was thankful
this wasn't the first time for him to be on the jungle
floor. It's like nothing you'd find anywhere else.

It had been 20 minutes since Pete had ejected, and he
figured it would be another 10 or 20 before the Jolly
Green rescue choppers could be in the area. So as
he got out his card with the code words for that day.
Each day during the mission briefing, flight crews were
given code words for the day that changed every day,
allowing flight crew members to report in without fear
of eavesdropping. "Mayday. Mayday. Mayday. This is
Bot 16. Bot 16 on Guard Channel. I am Gringo Alpha
[healthy and moving] Angels plus 1 [2 kilometers

plus 1 kilometer] November [north] from crash site. Condition Delta [no enemy sighted]. Over."

"Roger, Bot 16. This is Knife 21. Copy. Jolly Green is 18 minutes out. Do you copy?"

"Roger. Got it." Pete could hear a jet overhead but couldn't see it due to the jungle canopy. He planned to keep moving north until the Jolly got into the area. His heart was beating like a hammer, but he still had not heard or made any sighting of the enemy. He did hear a dog barking off in the distance behind him and hoped it wasn't tracking him. A GI in the jungle stood out like a diamond in a goat's butt. The after-shave, the bath soap, the shoe polish and even the foods they ate gave off an odor or fragrance that was so unique to the jungle that their presence could be detected a quarter of a mile downwind. Most combatants like Pete refused to use deodorants and colognes and limited the soap use on themselves and their clothes to the bland white soap provided by the DoD for just that reason.

Pete soon came to a small clearing in the jungle and figured this would be a good place for a helicopter to pick him up. He found a good hiding place in a bamboo grove just off the clearing and crawled in for the wait for Jolly. He pulled out his pen-gun flare and loaded it to signal Jolly and checked his .38 to be ready to fire. He always kept an empty chamber under the hammer to ensure it didn't discharge accidentally during ejection. It was ready and safety off, with a ball round in firing position. It wasn't much of a jungle gun, but it was what he was issued and about all he could carry in his survival vest. Some pilots claimed to save the last round for themselves if capture was eminent. Pete never bought into that, for he wasn't ever going to be captured…or at least wasn't planning on it. Now he wasn't so sure.

"Bot 16, this is Bot 18. Do you read me?" It was Dave.

"Read you loud and clear, buddy. What are doing over here?"

"Heard you were in trouble. But don't worry, We'll get you out of there. Jolly is only about ten minutes out now. Any enemy action around you?"

"Haven't seen or heard anything. But they might be waiting for a bigger fish. Watch yourself." Pete saw Bot 18 fly by through the clearing in the canopy. No enemy reaction yet. The Commies would wait, if they knew they had a downed pilot, for the rescue forces to arrive before opening up with their AAA. They were very patient and would wait quietly for the fighters to make their low passes and then for the helicopters to come in before reacting with their intense ground fire. They'd rather take out a fighter than a crummy chopper, but would take what they could get. It was a trap they had used successfully several times before. And they really did not care if they got the pilot or not, dead or alive, as they had enough POWs for their political purposes. They wanted the downed pilot to stay free and moving, for they knew the Americans would risk all to keep one of their own from being captured.

In the distance, Pete could hear the sounds of props and rotors. It had to be the Jolly Greens with their A-1 escorts. "Bot 16, this is Jolly Zero One. Do you read?"

"Loud and clear, Jolly. Get me out of here."

"Will do, Bot, but I need for you to give me the verification code numbers first." These were numbers, like the code words of the day, that only an Allied pilot would know from their mission briefing.

Pete couldn't find his card. He must have dropped it in the jungle. "How stupid," he thought. "I can't find it, Jolly. I can't find the son of a bitch." Panic was seeping in. Pete knew they wouldn't come in if they thought this was a trap and he was really a gook trying to sucker them in.

"No problem, Bot 16. I have a couple of questions for you." They always kept six questions on file to which only you would know the answer. "What kind of a motorcycle do you own, Bot 16?"

"Can-Am. A Can-Am Spyder!" Pete shouted into the radio.

"Sweet, Bot 16. And your favorite sports team?"

"Air Force Academy Falcons!"

"Okay, Bot 16. You're lucky we're not Navy Rescue. Boys, we got us a rescue to do. Bot 16, give me a flare."

Pete fired his pen-gun flare, and two red balls of fire streaked up through the clearing. Now everyone in the neighborhood would know where he was. The A-1s streaked across the clearing with guns firing, looking for any enemy reaction. There was none. Then they came back around much slower, again firing down into the jungle. No response. They began dropping canisters of CS gas into the surrounding jungle abeam and downwind of Pete's position.

Pete figured the choppers would be next, so he left his hiding place in the bamboo and ran out into the middle of the clearing. He could hear explosions in the distance, probably the fighters attacking known gun positions in the area or just diversion to keep the Commies' heads down. He really didn't care. He had others things going on in his life just now.

"Bot 16, give me smoke."

Pete popped open a canister of orange smoke. It helped the chopper to find him and gave them the direction of the wind. The first chopper made a high speed pass over the clearing firing his mini-guns randomly into the surrounding jungle as the second chopper started his approach to pick up Pete.

All the gun fire must have made one of the gook gunners nervous as he returned machine gun fire at the H-3. Then all hell broke loose. A quad ZPU high upon the ridge to the east opened up on one of the A-1s, and two 37mm guns started firing on the fighters. Individual rifles and machine guns started popping off all round Pete. The choppers returned fire as best they could, but this was no environment for either prop or rotor. "Abort. Abort. Abort." came the call over Pete's radio. And just as suddenly as they had appeared, the A-1s and the choppers were gone. They could not survive against such AAA. They would have to let the fighters soften up the area before trying again.

Pete scrambled back to his hiding place in the bamboo thicket. This was truly an "Oh Shit" moment. He knew he was in trouble now.

The fighters took on the 37mm positions with missiles, and their firing stopped. But they couldn't exactly determine the location of the ZPU, which was now quiet. The fighters and the A-1s put ordinance all along the ridge line, but the ZPU continued to fire sporadically.

Pete didn't know what to do. He was surrounded by the enemy. They knew his location. And the area was too hot for a rescue. It wasn't even noon yet, so he couldn't expect to have the cover of night to help him. He was screwed. He was about out of options. Then it got worse.

* * *

21

From his hiding place, Pete could see a line of enemy soldiers approaching his position…bayonets fixed on their rifles…same situation to his rear. They were firing into clumps of bushes and into any possible hiding place. They were obviously looking for him, and they had him totally surrounded. Pete picked up his emergency radio for one last call…"Whiskey. Tango. Foxtrot. Repeat. Whiskey. Tango. Foxtrot. Over." This was the coded message to notify rescuers that capture or death was imminent. He had just called off his own rescue since he knew what was about to occur.

Pete had a choice to make, which was really no choice at all. He could start shooting at the enemy and perhaps kill or wound at best five of them…and expect to be shot in return. He could save the last bullet for himself. Or he could surrender and try his escape later. Pete had never been a quitter, and even though he might lose this battle, he could still win the war. He thought seriously about surrender. But then he had always said he'd rather be dead than a POW. He knew if he started firing at the enemy soldiers, surely one of them would do the job for him…and that's what he did.

"God, forgive me." Pete stood up and squeezed off the five rounds in his .38, fully expecting to die immediately. Surprisingly to Pete, no one returned fire. They were going to take him alive.

He smashed his emergency radio with the handle of his .38 so it wouldn't fall into the hands of the Commies. He quickly swallowed one of the three-day compasses and drank his last water.

He pulled the bright orange signal panel from the pocket of his flight suit, held it above his head, and slowly stood back up…still hoping one of the enemy soldiers would get trigger-happy and finish him off. There was a lot of shouting as the soldiers surrounded the clump of bamboo. Pete had just become a statistic.

As Pete emerged from the bamboo thicket with his hands above his head, he was surrounded by a dozen or more of the enemy, all with bayonets pointed toward him. There was a lot of discussion among them, none of which Pete could understand. He still did not understand their lack of reaction to his .38 volley, and no one seemed to be taking charge of his capture. They just continued to look at Pete and talk among themselves.

Finally, after about 15 of the longest minutes of his life, what appeared to be an officer approached Pete and his captors. "Good morning, Lieutenant. We have been waiting for you." Pete didn't understand that comment, but did not respond. "Please remove your vest and empty your pockets." Pete was in no position to argue and complied. "Now please drop your flight suit to your ankles." They took all of his survival equipment …even that which he had hidden in his uniform, his money belt, and of course, his big watch. Curiously, they did not examine his boots and allowed him to keep them on.

"Lieutenant, we are going to take a short walk. As you have found, the jungle is difficult to penetrate, so I will leave your hands untied. The soldier behind you will be holding the rope being tied around your neck. It will be in your best interest not to resist. Follow me."

Pete still did not fully understand what was occurring. Why the formal treatment? He fully expected torture or at least something much worse than what he had received. This was nothing like what was taught at Snake School. He was ready for the worst, but they were treating him like a special guest. He just didn't get it.

Their journey finally took them to a jungle trail and then to a jeep trail. The walking was certainly easier. There was still no opportunity to escape. He was seriously outnumbered and outgunned. He called out to his captor and told him he needed to take a piss, wondering just how much English this guy knew. "Help yourself," he offered, pointing off the side of the trail. He went, but with his rope handler and three gooks with bayonets. "Well, that didn't get me anywhere," he thought.

Further along the trail, they passed a 37mm gun position. This might have been one of them firing earlier. The gunners were obviously joking about him as they chided him and laughed. One of the fuse cutters flipped him a thumbs up.

After about an hour's trek, they arrived at a military compound compete with barbed wire fence topped with concertina wire, an armed watch tower and gun bunkers. Inside the compound were several buildings constructed of bamboo. It looked like something out of an old war comic book. One of the guards on duty saluted Pete's captor, so he figured him to be someone of authority.

Pete followed his captor into the first building, followed by three armed soldiers. The officer directed him into a bamboo cell and chained the door. All Pete knew was that he was still alive and uninjured. His thoughts were on escape. His cage was about a six-foot cube, with floors, walls and ceiling made of bamboo. The officer sat behind a small desk and spoke something into a hand-cranked phone. Shortly, one of the soldiers brought him a pot of tea. Pete noticed that there were two cups. The officer poured one and offered it to Pete. He had flashbacks to Snake School. He did not respond. "Come now, Lieutenant. You need not be rude. Korean tea is very good."

"My God," thought Pete. "Are they really going to play 'good cop, bad cop' on me? I don't think I want to meet the Bad Cop. This ain't going to be pretty."

"You may wonder why you are being treated so well, Lieutenant. This is not at all like they taught you in the Philippines, is it? They probably told you that we were some slant-eyed Barbarians that would cut off your testicles and shove bamboo sticks up under your fingernails. Right?"

Pete still not respond.

"Okay, Lieutenant, let's save the conversation. I am the District Commandant here, and you will find my English impeccable. I was raised near LA and attended USC. I returned here to help my people fight this war of liberation from Western control and intervention. We defeated you in the early '50s, but we did not finish the job. Now that we in the north are stronger, our leaders have chosen this time to reunite our country. No longer are you fighting a rag-tag army aided by our Chinese brothers. Now you are facing a highly equipped, modern and efficient Korean military force determined and dedicated to force you off our peninsular forever. The 38th parallel will soon disappear, and we will all be one nation again. The Western forces, as usual, are not prepared to fight this sort of extended warfare and as in your Viet Nam intrusion, you will soon tire of the continuous deaths of your GIs and will tuck your tails and leave. You Americans are soft and lazy. I can never understand why you even get involved. Your leaders, unlike ours, are idiots controlled by greed and big business. Your effort here in Korea is doomed. Our people's revolution will continue and will force you into the sea...once again.

"And I know all I need to know about you... and that is that you are an American pilot who flies an airplane with a small wingman. There is something that you may not know. Unfortunately for you, there is a bounty on your head. We have friends who want to talk with you and learn more about it...and they will pay me well for you. Ironically enough, you are going to pay for my son's education...of course at USC. Bizarre, isn't it? I want to keep you safe and healthy until they arrive."

Now Pete understood. He was of great personal value to his captor. Now he had to factor that into his plan to escape.

* * *

22

Once he heard Pete's final Whiskey Tango Foxtrot call, Dave became frantic. His best friend had just been captured by the Commies, and there was nothing he could do about it. His whole adult life, as short as it had been, had included Pete, both looking out for each other, each watching the other's six o'clock. Once the Jolly Greens had cleared out of the area, he flew back in and checked out the area. He had to stay high to stay away from the AAA and was way too high to see what was going on around the bamboo grove below. He could still see Pete's parachute hung in the jungle canopy, but he had no idea what had happened. What Pete still alive? Was he again on the run? He knew Pete would try to escape. Questions and concerns and fears ran through Dave's mind. He felt so helpless. His friend was probably less than a mile away from him, and there was nothing he could do. Or was there?

Dave headed back to Taegu. The 45 minutes passed quickly, but by the time he had landed, cleared his debriefing and checked in his survival gear, his plan was clear. He headed straight for the computer room at Bot Ops and opened up the software that drove his robotic wingman and his fighter's computer. He copied the robot's RTB, return to base, procedures and drug it into his fighter's software. He rechecked it to ensure that both robot and fighter could return to Taegu without him and land safely. Air Force was going to be pissed enough at him if, no, when he initiated his plan. He was going after Pete, and his fighter was going to get him there.

Dave checked tomorrow's schedule, and he was scheduled to takeoff at 0600. He had a lot to do before then. He ate a good dinner at the Mess. It might be his last for a while. Then he took his malaria tablet and swallowed his three-day compass. He tried to sleep that night, but the best he could muster was to watch the hands on the clock at the end of his bunk go around five or six times. He finally got up and studied the topo map for that area, just in case he and Pete could escape and evade. He started to write a short note to somebody to tell them what he was going to do, but he couldn't think of anyone to send it to. This is as lonely as Dave had ever felt. He was among his comrades who would die for him, but with Pete captured and enduring the associated pain and fear, he couldn't, and wouldn't, let it go.

His plan included getting Pete and him back to safety. He taped a rubber topo map to his right thigh and an emergency radio to his left. He was hoping that if the Commies caught him, they would not strip search him. He re-checked his money belt for the ring saw, matches, the Pointee-Talkee and a rubber water bag. That's all he could do. He was ready.

He loaded the modified software into his fighter and headed out for his own personal war.

Take-off and departure were normal, and he was soon back in the area where Pete was shot down. He finally obtained a visual on Pete's chute still in the tree tops. He had to make this look good for both the Air Force and the enemy. It had to look as if he were just doing his normal search-and-destroy thing, so he notified Ops that he had acquired truck traffic and was initiating an attack. He and his robot rolled in and fired at these imaginary targets and received some return AAA fire. As he positioned for his last run, he commanded his robot to return to base and started down. At 7500 feet, Dave commanded his fighter to RTB and blew off his canopy. At least Air Force would get their plane back. At 5000 feet, he ejected.

He got a clean opening of his chute and performed his four-line riser cut, steering it toward the small clearing where Pete was captured. Dave didn't know if he would be captured or not, but he was ready either way. If he did get captured, he would most likely end up near Pete...and that might be the easiest way to find him.

Dave thought the jungle below was unusually quiet... as though he really had anything to compare it to. Everything looked so peaceful, and the only noise was the flapping of his chute canopy. The wind was stronger than Dave had first estimated, and Dave was not going to be able to make it to the clearing. He crossed his legs just before penetrating the jungle canopy. His landing was terrible. His parachute did not snag limbs as he had expected. He hit several big limbs on the way to the ground. And he landed on his side. The pain in his left shoulder was incredible. He had dislocated it.

He struggled to get his parachute harness off, which is very difficult to do with one arm. The pain was overwhelming, and Dave felt as if he were going to pass out. He tried to stand, but instead dropped to his knees. Dave didn't know if he were dreaming or unconscious. His head was swirling just as it had done in the boxing ring years before at the Academy. Part of his brain was working; the rest was unconscious. He sensed people around him speaking in a language he could not understand. Suddenly, the feeling of water in his face and in his mouth brought his brain back up on line. He was laying on the jungle floor surrounded by enemy soldiers carrying rifles with bayonets. They had stripped him of his survival vest and everything he had taped to his body. He knew this was not going well, and he, like Pete, had just become a statistic.

"Lieutenant, this must be my lucky day. Can you stand up?" Dave shook his head to clear it. The pain in his shoulder was severe. He got to his knees and then to his feet. "If you will follow me, we will try to get you some medical help. Please do not resist my men or try to escape. With your injuries, I don't think it would be pleasant or successful for you to try."

Walking was difficult for Dave, with his injured shoulder, but after a short while, they arrived at the same compound where they were holding Pete. The District Commandant directed Dave to sit on the steps of the porch. "Wait here while I summon our medical sergeant." Soon, another soldier appeared, carrying a small drab bag. Without speaking, the medical sergeant pulled out a pair of scissors to remove Dave's flight suit. The Commandant stopped him. He did not want to destroy Dave's uniform. Dave didn't understand that, but he had greater things to worry about. By unzipping the flight suit and with a bit of discomfort, they were able to expose Dave's shoulder. The medic reset the shoulder and taped it down to Dave's ribs.

Pete had heard Dave's cries of pain during the resetting process and recognized his voice. But when Dave entered the cell, he did not make eye contact or show any signs of recognition.

"Gentlemen, I will let you two do the introductions. You can tell your new roommate all the things I have told you. I am going to my dinner. If you need anything, ask these guards. They do not speak English, but they will come and get me. Good afternoon." And with that, the Commandant left the office with two guards standing watch.

"Dave, what the hell are you doing here?"

"I came to rescue you, buddy." For a brief moment, they just stared at each other, then broke into thunderous laugher. "I'm sure you would do the same for me. Right?"

"Never in a million years. You are nuts!"

Pete told Dave about the Commandant and the bounty. "Surely, there is some way we can use that. And we'd better do it soon because it sounds as if someone is coming to get us."

"Well, the good news is that they want to keep us in good shape and healthy. Who ever wants us must want us in one piece. Herr Commandant wouldn't even let the medic cut off my uniform. I don't get it. No torture, no harassment, no nothing. I just don't get it."

"A little grub would be nice."

"Yeah, maybe some fish head soup or maybe some nice rat jambalaya."

"With fried roach appetizers."

The setting sun laid down long shadows across the floor of the room. Through hand signals, Pete communicated to one of the guards that he wanted water. He soon returned with a pot of hot tea and two cups. He figured correctly that hot tea would be purer than any water they might come up with. Soon the two guards were replaced by two others, one of whom was carrying a small black bucket filled with hot coals. Not only did it cut the cool of the night air, but it gave a dim glow to the room. No other lights were visible in the camp...a total blackout. But Pete and Dave could hear lots of lively conversation and occasional laughter...probably no different from the Allied camps to the south. Escape would be difficult...even more so now with Dave's bummed shoulder.

* * *

23

Pete and Dave were awakened just at daybreak by the sound of helicopter blades. They grew louder, and they could tell when it landed nearby and shutdown. "Probably a re-supply chopper," Dave offered.
"I thought we had about stopped all of that."

"Good morning, gentlemen," greeted the Commandant. He was accompanied by a dozen of his gorillas, all with bayonets attached. They seemed to have a thing about bayonets there. "I hope you slept well. It's not the best accommodations, but we only offer the best to our longer term visitors. You will be leaving us this morning. Our friends to the north are here to pick you up."

"Do you want to tell us what the hell you are talking about?"

"Well, as I mentioned earlier. There is a bounty on your heads…because of the cute little airplane that flies as your wingman. Both our Chinese brothers and the Russians are wanting more info on this technology and are offering a reward for each of you we provide them. You are special since you are numbers one and two to be captured alive. Congratulations."

"You can't do that", argued Dave. "It's against the Geneva Conventions. We're Prisoners of War and demand to be treated as such."

The Commandant laughed. "Lieutenant, you don't really want to be treated the way we treat POWs. Believe me. We don't need any more of your pilots filling our prison compounds. We have all we need for our purposes. With your busted shoulder, we would have just put you in a cell and let you die. It's only because of your value to our friends that you received any medical aid. The Geneva Conventions don't mean anything to us. We didn't sign it and don't give a damn about it. So you are really better off. The bad news for you is that neither the Chinese nor the Russians can ever admit they have you. That would be against your Geneva Conventions," he mused. "Once they are through with you, they will have to make you disappear."

"Oh, and to make your day just a little brighter, the Chinese don't want the Russians to get you, and the Russians don't want the Chinese to get you. Neither wants the other to gain an upper hand in this technology. And in this bidding for your bodies and your knowledge, the Russians won. They offered more. Did I say thank you? So the Chinese will probably try to keep you from getting to Russian territory. The Russian airbase at Vladivostok is only three or four hours up the coast from here via helicopter, so it should be an

Return to Stanley Canyon

exciting ride. I have already been paid, so it matters little to me whether you make it or not. However, if the Chinese shoot you down, it will just keep the bidding going. Hmmm."

The Commandant unlocked the chain on the door to the cell and motioned for Dave and Pete to follow the guards.

They exited the compound and traversed a narrow jungle path for about a hundred yards to a clearing where awaited a large drab green helicopter with a red star insignia. The helicopter was similar in size and design of the Sikorsky H-3 cargo chopper, with a side door and a rear ramp. Two pilots in Russian flight gear and what must have been two flight mechanics awaited.

The flight mechs, via hand gestures, directed Pete and Dave up the ramp and into the helicopter. The left side of the cargo bay was lined with about fifteen red nylon troop seats with their backs to the left side of the fuselage. At the front of the cargo bay was a narrow passage way that led to the flight deck. The pilots had already squeezed through there and were going through the pre-flight checklist. Strapped down to the floor of the helicopter just aft of the right side door was a stretcher with a body on it. They could tell from the uniform, it was an American pilot, but the face was covered with bandages, and there was a cast on his left arm and more bandages on his right leg. Pete recalled what the Commandant had said about injured American pilots receiving medical aid. The Russians must have wanted this pilot, too, but Pete could tell

207

by the insignia on his flight suit that he was not from the Bot Squadron. He neither spoke nor moved nor acknowledged Pete or Dave in any fashion. They couldn't attest to his even being alive.

The flight mechs reminded Pete of what he had always thought Russians soldiers would look like...dirty and big and mean...the kind of guys you would want on your side in a rugby scrum. He knew he didn't want to mess with these guys, but he was still thinking about escape.

He noticed Dave was really playing up his injury... walking all stooped over and nursing his shoulder with his right hand. He knew Dave well enough to know he was thinking escape, too. But they were out manned and out gunned, again, inside an enemy helicopter with wounded comrades, heading on a one-way trip to Russia...if the Chinese don't get them first.

One of the Russian hulks pushed Pete back into a troop seat and fastened his lap belt. He grabbed one wrist and then the other and secured them together with a plastic tie. He yanked it so hard, Pete thought it would cut off the circulation. To avoid the same treatment, Dave sat down in a troop seat one down from Pete. The other mech fastened his lap belt. Dave figured that since he had only one good hand, they didn't secure it. One mech strapped in several seats forward of Dave. The other sat on the floor aft of the stretcher, leaning back against his large tool box. They left the aft ramp and the cargo door open, probably for ventilation.

The pilots started the turbines and engaged the rotors. Once they had completed the pre-flight checklist, they pulled the chopper into a hover and started their take-off run. Next stop...Vladivostok, Russia.

The inside of a military helicopter can be very noisy. The cargo bay is directly beneath the engines and the main rotor transmission, and all sound-proofing is removed to expose any combat damage and to allow easy access to the flight mechs for inspections and repair. This was no exception. The noise was especially loud for Dave and Pete, for they were used to wearing helmets with headsets. But there was no ear protection or helmet for any of the five passengers.

Dave and Pete were seated with their backs to the left side of the fuselage, looking out the open cargo door. The flight mech to Dave's left was dozing. The other was reading a copy of a Russian newspaper. Dave had forgotten most of the Russian he had learned at the Academy, but he could read its name, Red Star. He had learned just enough to get a B in class, and that was good enough at the time. Now he wished he had studied a bit harder.

From the shadows cast across the floor of the helicopter, Pete figured they were flying east. When they hit the Sea of Japan, they turned left slightly to follow the coast. They had stayed below a thousand feet thus far, perhaps fearing Chinese interception. The border between Russia and Korea is less than 100km long, which meant the Chinese Air Force was always only a few minutes away. The mountains along the coast were probably giving them some protection from Chinese radar.

When he finished reading his paper, the flight mech folded it up and threw it at the dozing mech. He picked it up from the cabin floor and thanked him in Russian, "Spa ceba". The flight mech began rummaging around in his tool box again and pulled out a brown paper bag holding a clear bottle with no label and filled with a clear liquid…and took a long swig. Pete figured it to be vodka. When the other mech noticed this, he shouted out to his friend over the noise of the chopper. He obviously wanted a draw. They would each take a drink, screw on the lid and pitch it back and forth to each other. Soon, it began taking its effect, and they began to make a game of how close they could get to Dave's face with the empty bottle, hitting him on several occasions. Dave continued to favor his injury and protect his shoulder and his face. The game continued. The vodka was kicking in.

The mech fished around in his tool box and came out with a large Crescent wrench. They continued their game of how close they could get to Dave's face, but now with the wrench, once or twice grazing him. The flight mechs were having a grand time at Dave's expense. When he tired of the wrench, one mech opened a case attached to the wall of the cargo bay and pulled out a hand grenade. Now they were getting serious…and drunker…and the game was getting very dangerous…and about over.

On its last pass by Dave's face, Dave grabbed the grenade with his good right hand, pulled its pin out with his teeth and spit it on the floor. Just for emphasis, he kicked the pin out the open cargo door. All he had to do was let the handle on the grenade pop off and in seven seconds, there would be an explosion.

Time seemed to stop in that helicopter bay. No one moved. Who would be the first to blink? The two flight mechs, even in their drunken stupor, seemed to think they needed to do something. Dave popped his seat belt loose, stood up, danced around waving his arm franticly in a wild frenzy, finally sticking the grenade in the face of the seated mech. Dave was acting like a hopeless crazy man, and maybe he was. Dave pointed at a parachute laying on the floor, then at the mech, and then at the open cargo door. The seated mech wasted no time donning the chute and bailing out.

The other mech was standing now, glaring at Dave, estimating his chances against a one-armed man holding a pinless grenade. He bullrushed Dave, but as he passed the litter, the bandaged pilot with his one good arm swept the feet out from under the mech, who then went sprawling to the floor. Dave smashed the butt of the grenade into his head and shoved the chuteless mech out the cargo door. He shoved the grenade into a butt can and threw it out the door, too.

The noise level in the cargo bay was almost deafening, so Dave figured the two pilots up front were clueless to what was going on in the back. With a pair of wire cutters from the tool box, Dave freed Pete. "Okay Superman, what do we do now?

"Give me a screwdriver, Pete." Dave shoved the screwdriver into the sole of Pete's flight boot and ripped off the heel, exposing the ring saw he had hidden there.

Pete, being the only one with two good arms, knew exactly what to do. "Dave, take this wrench and bang on the floor of the chopper. One of the pilots has to come back here and check it out. I'll be waiting for him with our little friend here."

Pete took a position hiding beside the passage forward to the flight deck. Dave began a staccato pounding with the wrench…and just as expected, the co-pilot in the left seat loosened his lap belt and started through the passage…with his pistol drawn. Dave hadn't figured on this. Just as the co-pilot was about to exit the passage, Dave pointed vigorously up at the transmission. When the Russian looked up in response, Pete wrapped the ring saw around the hand carrying the pistol and yanked with all his adrenaline in tact, cutting through the tendons, the muscle, the veins, arteries and everything else. The gun with the hand still attached fell to the floor, followed by the writhing pilot. Pete pushed him out the door. Commies 0, Zoomies 3…with one to go.

"Good job, dude. Got any ideas how to get the last one? We gotta hurry. He'll be looking for his co-pilot soon."

Pete held up the bloody ring saw. Dave shouted back over the noise of the chopper. "I don't think that will work. He might hit the flight controls if he struggles. Wait. I got an idea. Get out another grenade." Pete complied. "You are going to have to do this since you have two arms. Unscrew the top pin assembly from the body of the grenade."

"Are you crazy?"

"Just do it. I know what I'm doing...I think."

Pete unscrewed the top and separated it from the bottom.

"Now pull the pin and let the handle pop off." Pete looked at Dave, looking for some signs of assurance. He didn't get any. "When the handle comes off, it allows the firing pin to hit and set off the fuse. It burns down this tube until it ignites the powder in the base of the grenade. Now pop loose the handle."

Pete followed Dave's instructions...and he was right. Seven seconds after the handle left the grenade's top, the fuse burned all the way down the fuse tube and fizzled out. "How did you know that?" Pete demanded.

"I don't know why I knew it; I just knew it. Now put it all back together. What we have here is a dud! Now let's see what I can do with it. Keep your ring saw ready in case this doesn't work."

Dave took the grenade in his right hand and started toward the passage to the flight deck. Peeking into the cockpit, Dave saw that the remaining pilot was holding a map with both hands. That was good news, for the chopper had to be either on auto-pilot or the friction locks on the flight controls were holding them in place. In either event, the chopper would continue to fly itself for a while. The pilot was obviously startled when Dave slid into the co-pilot's seat holding a

213

grenade. Dave again pulled the pin with his teeth and held the grenade so the pilot could see. Dave pointed toward the pilot's chute he was wearing and then to the open cockpit window next to the pilot. The pilot protested in Russian. "Do svedanya moi droog," returned Dave, goodbye my friend, in the best Russian he could muster. And he let the handle spring away from the grenade and pitched the grenade under the pilot's seat but out of his reach. Without hesitation, the pilot unfastened his lap belt and rolled out the open cockpit window.

Pete slipped into the empty seat, shaking his head in total disbelief.

"Pete, why don't you get that grenade out of here...just in case I was wrong."

* * *

24

"I could sure stand a good cold beer, Dave. Remember that Jeep stuck on that boulder and how good that beer was. Probably the best I ever had."

"I remember some cut-off jeans and that tank top. Damn, she looked fine. That probably would have been some of the best I ever had."

"Okay, let's get our heads back in the game. Here we are heading straight at Russia, who would like to kill us. We're flying over North Korea, who would like to kill us, and we're trying to stay away from the Chinese, who would like to kill us. And you want to talk about tank tops? And we're in an airplane that neither of us knows how to fly...and we don't have a clue where the hell we are."

"Well, I know we took off back there for a three to four flight...and that was an hour ago. So we must have about two or three hours of fuel left...or more. We're probably good there. These look like the fuel gauges, but everything's written in Russian...and

I can't read Russian very well. Maybe I should have paid more attention in class back at the Academy. But the first thing we'd better do is to head straight out to sea and find the US Navy. Turn right perpendicular to the coast and check the heading on the whiskey compass. We'll just keep on that heading until…"

"Until what?" asked Pete.

"I don't know yet. Work in progress."

"And I don't know how to fly a helicopter. Do you? What do you think this big lever beside the seat is for? It looks important."

"It is important," answered Dave. "But we don't need to move it right now. Just turn. It flies just like an airplane when you're at cruise speed."

"And just how do you know this? Are you BS-ing me again, Dave?"

"Well, there was this girl in Phoenix."

"Oh, give me a break."

"No, really. When I was in Flight School at Willie, I dated this girl whose dad was a doctor. And he owned a chopper, a Robinson R-22. It was a little bitty thing. Well, he didn't have a lot of hours and wanted to have me fly with him as he learned to fly that thing. All in all, I got about 10 hours of stick time. I never soloed, but I felt pretty comfortable in it. So while we're looking for the Navy, I'll give you some instruction… free."

"I only have a good right arm," continued Dave, "so I will fly the stick, and you can use this lever. It's called the collective pitch...or just the pitch lever. Every time I say pitch up or pitch down, you move it up or down one quarter inch...no more; no less. If I say pitch up three times, pull it up three-fourths of an inch. If you can do that, I think we can fly this thing."

"All right, this stick is called the cyclic in a helicopter, and it performs pretty much like the stick in our jets. Move it right and we bank right. Pull it back and the nose comes up. Real simple...as long as we have plenty of airspeed. It works differently when we get in a hover, but I'll take care of that when it happens."

"The easy way to think of it is that the rotor blades create a thrust vector. And remember that a vector has both magnitude and direction. Now the big lever in your left hand is called the collective pitch, and that's what it does. It collectively changes the pitch on each of the blades and changes the amount of thrust. You control the magnitude of the thrust vector."

"Now what my stick does is to point that vector. I move my stick to the right, the vector points to the right, and we turn right. So you control the length of the thrust vector, the amount of thrust, and I control the direction it points. Nothing to it, right?"

"I can do my part," Pete offered with some reluctance. "Now let's go find the Navy."

Pete and Dave got the chopper pointed out to sea and held a heading of 115°. Together they descended to

Glenn Coleman

several hundred feet above the water to keep under
Chinese and now Russian radar. They continued to
cruise at 215 km per hour. Dave performed a few turns
just to get the feel of the chopper, but he kept heading
southeast. After about an hour, they figured they were
about 125 miles off shore and out of danger from the
bad guys. Now they had to find the good guys...or help
the good guys find them.

Neither Pete nor Dave knew how to use the radio or
the IFF since it was all different equipment and all in
Russian. The international signal for distress was to
fly in a triangle, so they climbed up to 1000 meters on
the altimeter and flew continual one-minute legs of a
triangle. Surely, the Navy would pick them up on radar
and come to take a look.

After about twenty minutes of this, Pete and Dave
were beginning to think this might not have been an
effective plan. What else could they do? They figured
they had about a hour and a half of fuel left. They
couldn't ditch in the ocean since they had the injured
pilot on board. He would certainly drown. And Dave
was in no condition to swim. They started thinking
about heading back for land. Where the hell is the
Navy? And then their bad condition got worse.

Out Pete's window appeared a jet, a Korean MiG,
with flaps down, nose high, trying to stay in formation
with the chopper to take a look. After three or four
minutes, the MiG fired a burst of cannon fire straight
ahead, the signal for them to turn around and head
back or be shot down. They considered diving down to
just above the water to evade the MiG, but figured any

evasive maneuver would bring immediate retaliation. They figured the only way to survive was to head back to land.

"Pete, take off your tee shirt and wave it to the MiG. Let him know we are giving up. We'll try to come up with something. I wonder if there's a rifle in back."

"I didn't see one," offered Pete. He waved his white shirt at the MiG while Dave started a slow left turn.

Pete was watching the MiG to see his reaction to the turn back toward shore when their luck suddenly improved. The MiG had been focusing on the Russian chopper and not checking his six o'clock. Tracers came in from behind the MiG and ripped off the right wing. The MiG did an immediate hard roll to the right and exploded just before it impacted the water. US Navy 1. MiG 0.

Sliding up into position on both sides of the chopper were two Navy A-4 fighters. "Glory Halleluiah!" Pete was waving frantically with his white shirt. He could only imagine the pilot's radio message back to the Air Boss on his carrier. "Uh, Flight Ops, we got a Russian helio with a guy hanging out the cockpit window waving what looks like a tee shirt." Pete had to come up with some plan to let the swabbies know they were Americans. He locked down the friction on the pitch lever to keep it in position and unfastened his lap belt and shoulder harness. "Uh, Flight Ops, the guy with the tee shirt just got out of the pilot's seat, went to the cargo bay door and mooned me. Repeat, mooned me. Over."

As Pete returned to the cockpit, Dave said, "Great, Pete, now as soon as they stop laughing, they'll probably shoot us down."

Both A-4s pulled slightly ahead of the chopper, turned right about 30° and sped away. They circled and came by again on that new heading. "They must want us to turn to that heading," suggested Dave and began his turn. The A-4s made one more pass and disappeared into the ocean's haze.

Pete and Dave had held the new heading of 145° for about 20 minutes when they were intercepted by an orange and white Navy helio. It flew up into position on Pete's side and waved back when Pete again waved his tee shirt. Then they pulled up on Dave's side to take a look. "Dave, they've got their mini-guns pointed right at us. Don't piss them off. They still think we are bad guys."

"Do something to show them we're Americans, Pete."

"Hell, I've already mooned them. What's more American than that? I'm all out of American flags and baseball cards."

The Navy chopper pulled ahead of Pete and Dave and banked his fuselage slightly to the left and right, the formation signal to join up information. Dave responded and felt a bit more comfortable. But the mini-gun was still pointed at his cockpit. They descended to about twenty feet above the water. "Pete, be ready with the pitch. This is where I really need you, buddy."

"Dave, over there at ten o'clock, what is that?"

"It looks like a destroyer. I'm getting sea sick looking at it. We must be in the middle of a battle group. Jesus, look at the carrier dead ahead."

"They're slowing down. Oh my God, we're going to have to hover this thing, Pete. Pitch up. Pitch up." Pete raised the lever slightly. "Pitch up." Dave finally got it into an uncomfortable hover.

Two more helios joined the hovering circus, one on each side. The pilot of the second Navy chopper pointed down into the water. They wanted Dave to ditch at sea. There were Navy divers standing in the doors of both additional choppers.

"We can't do that. We got our guy in the back." Pete pointed vigorously at the carrier. He screamed, "We gotta land on the carrier."

"They can't hear you, Pete."

The Navy continued to point into the water. There was no way they were going to allow that Russian chopper to land on a Navy carrier. This might be some sort of a trick. This was the end of the road for this chopper. It was ditch with the engines running or ditch when it ran out of fuel. Neither Pete nor Dave could leave the cockpit. It took them both to keep the chopper in the air. There was no way to communicate with the Navy choppers. The Navy pilot continued to point down into the water. Pete continued to point at the carrier.

A red signal light appeared from the bridge of the carrier...meaning Do Not Land. Then it began to flash white dots and dashes. Like most AF pilots, neither Pete nor Dave learned much Morse code in Flight School and remembered even less. But this gave Pete his answer. "I'm going to set the belly of this chopper in the water. Hang with me."

Pete pulled the fire extinguisher from the cockpit bulkhead and started beating on the window frame so the Navy pilot could see him. The Navy chopper was obviously in communications with the carrier's bridge. Pete and the Navy pilot were on the same wave-length, and he knew what Pete had in mind. After about 30 seconds of this, the Navy pilot flipped him a thumbs-up. The carrier's sonar was picking up Pete's signal through the water.

Pete started beating out tap code: 4,4 [T]-2,3 [H]-4,2 [R]-1,5[E] 1,5[E]-1,1 [A]-2,1[F]-3,5 [P]-3,4 [O]-5,2 [W]-4,3 [S]-4,4 [T]-5,2 [W]-3,4 [O]-5,2 [W]-3,4 [O]-4,5 [U]-3,3 [N]-1,4 [D]-1,5 [E]-1,4 [D]

After a short pause, the light from the carrier's bridge flashed back: 2,2 [G] 2,4 [I]-5,1 [V]-1,5 [E]-3,2 [M]-1,5 [E]-3,3 [N]-1,1 [A]-3,2 [M]-1,5 [E]-4,3 [S]

Pete returned: D-A-V-I-D-E-D-W-A-R-D-S-P-E-T-E-R-B-E-N-E-D-E-T-T-O

Pete looked at Dave, They didn't even know the name of the guy on the stretcher, and since they couldn't leave the flight controls, they didn't know how to get the information. But the guy on the stretcher had picked up the pistol from the floor and began answering himself by beating on the cabin floor.

J-O-H-N-C-H-A-R-L-E-S-S-T-E-B-I-N-S-K-I-U-S-A-I-R-F-O-R-C-E

Dave figured it out just a nanosecond ahead of Pete, and they shouted to each other in unison, "STEBINSKI?" "Oh shit," Dave repeated out of habit from years prior.

The Navy continued: G-I-V-E-M-E-F-A-V-O-R-I-T-E-S-P-O-R-T-S-T-E-A-M

"What are they saying," asked Dave. "I didn't get it."

"They are trying to verify we are who we say we are. They're asking security questions. Who's your favorite sports team? Mine's Air Force. Who's yours?"

"Send that!"

Air Force had seriously beaten Navy in football this year, and Pete was tempted to mention the Commander-in-Chief trophy. But this was no time to mess around. Here they were in a stolen chopper they could hardly fly, running out of fuel in the middle of the Sea of Japan, with injured on board, pleading for permission to land on a US Navy carrier. A-I-R-F-O-R-C-E-F-A-L-C-O-N-S, he tapped out.

It seemed forever for the carrier to answer. They were probably trying to figure out what to do. Hopefully, Pete thought, they were clearing the flight deck to give them a place to attempt a landing.

Finally, the red light from the carrier's bridge turned to green, and the ship's helios moved aside. The Navy chopper pilot flipped them a thumbs up for luck. It was obvious from Dave's erratic hovering that they were not chopper pilots.

The carrier was under way, and from the bow wave, Dave figured it to be a low speed, maybe 10-15 knots. This would help Dave, for with a bit of forward airspeed, this chopper would be easier to hover and land on the carrier's deck. Dave pushed forward on the stick and called for Pete to pull up on the pitch. They climbed up to about 1000 feet and swung around to a final approach on the carrier. Dave could tell from the flags that the ship was pointed into the wind.

They had, indeed, prepared the deck for the chopper's landing. The deck was totally void of airplanes and equipment...except for the tug about mid-ship to protect the ship's island from any debris in case they muffed this landing. The arresting barriers were up, perhaps to catch any crash debris or to snag the chopper if these two AF pilots couldn't get it on the deck safely. There was one lone swabbie on deck with paddles in raised hands to direct their landing. All was set for whatever was to come.

Dave rolled out on about a one-mile final to give Pete and Dave an opportunity to get fully in sync with their controls. Dave continued with his instructions to Pete. "I'm going to take it right down to the deck...no hovering. When you feel the wheels touch, begin to lower the pitch lever. Don't just jam it down, but lower it smoothly and keep it coming down. I'll keep it level with the stick. If we blow it, pull it back up to about where it is now...not all the way up. And we'll try to go around. But just small movements...and steady. Okay, pitch down, pitch down. Here we go. Too much. Pitch up. Okay, good."

Dave continued his directions all the way down final. The tower gave them a green light for approval to land, and then went dark. The ship looked huge and the man on the deck tiny. From their carrier/destroyer experience a few years earlier, Dave had hoped to never again set foot on a Navy ship. This one looked pretty damned good. "Thank God it's not another destroyer," Dave muttered to himself.

As they approached the stern of the carrier, they could feel the turbulence created by the boat's forward speed. Dave leveled off just a bit to get above it and pulled back on the stick a bit to slow his speed. The airspeed still showed positive in KM/HR, and Dave had no way to translate that. Nevertheless, all looked good. "Pitch down."

It were as if everything were in slow motion to Pete. He had never flown in a chopper and was not used to the low approach speeds. Dave continued on across the edge of the deck to his chosen landing spot. He could feel the presence of the deck below by the increased lift from the rotor. "Pitch down."

They were still in a slight descent, and finally both could feel the wheels begin the kiss the deck. Dave held it level. "Pitch down, Pitch down." The wheels were firmly touching the deck. "Slowly, pitch all the way down."

"Houston, the Eagle has landed!" Pete proudly announced.

"I don't know how to shut this son of a bitch down. Hold that lever all the way down until I figure this out, and keep your feet on the brakes."

From behind a barricade, a lone figure in flight gear ran out to the chopper and climbed in the cabin door. He was followed by four Marines carrying M-16's. Following them were several medics carrying stretchers and deck mechs pulling fire extinguishers. The Navy flight crewman entered the flight deck and without speaking began shutting down the helicopter's systems, taking the stick from Dave to keep the rotor system level, and applied the rotor brake when the blades had slowed down. Except for the sound of the flight instruments' gyros slowing down, everything was now as quiet as the deck of a carrier can be.

* * *

25

"Good job, plow boy," Stebinski offered. "At least you two queens stayed awake in flight school. Crappy landing, though. Thought I was going to have to come up there and do it for you."

"Shut up, you dumb Polack, or I will personally drag your stretcher outa here and throw it overboard."

"That's Captain Polack to you, Junior." Stebinski raised his good hand and shook Pete's and Dave's. "Thanks, guys. You saved my life. You two will always be my heroes. I guess I didn't do too bad of a job training you queens back at the Zoo." Dave and Pete just shook their heads. Some things never change. Some things will never be the same.

The first stop for the three Zoomies was the medical bay. The docs cleaned up Stebinski's injuries as best they could and checked out Dave's shoulder. After a shower and fresh clothing from the Navy, the ship's Captain stopped in for a visit and welcome aboard. "Gentlemen, we have contacted your units as to your conditions and are awaiting further instructions. Lieutenant Edwards, your commander told me a very interesting story as to how you got here. You must have balls of brass, but I wish we all had a friend like you. Amazing! By the way, your aircraft made it home safely…missing a few parts, such as an ejection seat and a canopy. But I guess it was a pretty fair trade since we got one of the Ruskies' new helicopters. We have already stowed it below deck to keep it out of view of the satellites. The Foreign Technology Division will be out to take it off our hands in a week or so. They are wanting to take it apart…especially these new engines."

Two intel teams came into the infirmary, one to debrief Stebinski and one for Pete and Dave. They wanted to know all the details about their POW experiences. Dave wondered if he should have a lawyer present just in case the Air Force planned to prosecute him for what he did. Whatever happens, it was worth it.

As usual, the Navy chow was excellent. "This sure beats the hell out of rats and roaches, doesn't it?" added Dave.

"Or cheap vodka and caviar. What do you think the Russians would have done with us if we had not escaped?" asked Pete. "I know they want to get info on the robotic wingmen, but I wonder how far they would have gone to get it. And what would they have done with us when they finished, when we were no longer of any value. I think we need to get that info back to our buddies in the squadron."

"I'm sure we will get our chance. I wonder why they wanted Stebinski."

Even on something as large as a carrier, billets are limited. Due to his injuries, they kept Stebinski in the Critical Care Unit. Dave and Pete bunked their one night in the medical bay.

The carrier was launching missions that night, and neither Dave nor Pete could sleep. They found their way to an outside observation deck just below the bridge to watch the launch operations and to enjoy the cool ocean breeze coming down the flight deck. They would get an occasional whiff of the jet exhaust or of the steam from the catapult.

"Think you could ever do that?" asked Dave.

"Launch off a carrier? I could, but I wouldn't like it."

"Can you imagine losing a engine on take-off and ditching or bailing out, knowing that this carrier was about to run over you? And the worst part is knowing that if everything goes right on your mission, that you still have to find your way back to this big boat and land."

"And if you make it back, you get to live on a steel island with 3000 other guys and be here for another year. I don't get it."

This small talk wasn't getting to the real question in Pete's heart. "Okay, Dave, I've just have to ask you this. What the hell were you doing? Why did you come after me? Believe me, I'm thankful you did...especially since everything worked out okay. But you risked everything...your plane, your Air Force career, your life. I honestly don't know if I would have done the same for you...and that bothers me."

"Yeah, you would have. If the roles had been reversed, you would have been there for me. I was overhead when they were trying to rescue you...and I just knew they would get you out. But when they couldn't, when you made that last call and went off the air, I knew exactly what I had to do. I know you well enough to know you would have tried everything you could do to escape, and I wanted to be there to help you do it. Really, what else could I do? If I had not tried, I would have had to spend the rest of my life wondering why. I would have been plagued with the what-ifs the rest of my life. I would have been second-guessing 'til the day I died. What choice did I have? And when I bailed out over you the next day, I didn't know if I would be taken as a POW or just sneaking through the jungle trying to find you and get you back. But things worked out alright...even with this shoulder. God was looking out for both of us. I know that's true."

"Well, Dave, you're one hell of a guy. They ought to make a movie about you, or at least, a statue, or maybe name a bridge after you."

"Naw, it's all about me. It's a selfish thing. Good friends are hard to find...and I got you trained just the way I like you. It's too hard to get another friend. This was just the easy way out."

"Okay, I get it," said Pete. "But do you understand just how close we came?"

"Sure I do, buddy, but this is what it's all about. This is what makes us different from the other cats. I went back to my high school reunion last year. There were still guys talking about the football game we played with Mt. Pleasant our senior year. We lost the game and lost our chance to make the play-offs. But some guys were talking about it as if it happened yesterday. Honestly, I don't even remember the game. If I were to go back and tell them about this day we had today, they'd stare at me blankly and go back to talking football. It would be like I was talking a foreign language. But this is what our lives are. We're a different breed of cat now. We live in a different orbit and will always live in a different orbit...for better or for worse."

"But Dave, don't you just love it?"

"Buddy, I wouldn't have it any other way." He punched Pete in the shoulder.

Pete was silent for a while, just watching the Navy jets launch and disappear into the night. He thought to himself, "I hope you guys have a guardian angel like I do." He knew he didn't deserve to be there. He should have died, or at least be a POW somewhere. Why did he survive? Why did everything go exactly right? Did the fates have something in mind for him? Many questions laid heavy on his mind.

The following day, a courier S2F would pick up Pete for a return to his home base at Taegu. After a debriefing, he would be flying missions again within two or three days. Dave and Stebinski would head for the big hospital at Tachikawa in Japan.

* * *

26

The distance from Taegu, Korea to Tachikawa was like crossing Texas, but Japan was an entirely different world...especially the pristine AF base hospital and grounds at Tachi. The staff was a mix of American and Japanese and treated their injured combatants like royalty. The patients all wore a hospital "uniform" that identified them as they went onto the main base for shopping or just exercise. They were not allowed to leave the base but had total freedom other than that. Dave especially loved the little sidewalk shop that baked sticky buns each morning. And the French Onion Soup at the Officers' Club was worth asking for the recipe. He certainly enjoyed the break but was growing anxious to return to the war. The medical staff had done a fine job on his shoulder, and with each day of therapy, it grew stronger and stronger. Dave was glad to be back in Air Force hands where he could speak the language and recognize the rank and insignia.

Dave would stop by to visit Stebinski every day, and he, too, was improving. His broken arm needed to be reset, and the burns on his face and legs were clean and healing. He was not a good patient. He, too, wanted to get back to his war, but the wait was to be longer for him due to the seriousness of his injuries. Dave wondered silently if Stebinski would ever get back on flight status. There was no question in Stebinski's mind. He would go kick some Korean butt tomorrow if they would let him.

After a week at Tachikawa, Dave still had not heard from his unit back at Taegu. Pete had written that he was back to flying daily missions and that everyone was asking about Dave and talking about their adventures. Dave's curiosity about his future finally drove him to call back to Taegu to talk to his Squadron Commander. The PACAF operator had no trouble ringing his office.

Kim, his Korean secretary, answered. "Colonel Malone's office."

"Hey, Miss Kim, this is Lieutenant Dave Edwards, calling from Japan. Can I talk to the Colonel?"

"Certainly, David. He's been wanting to talk with you. Hold, please."

"Colonel Malone."

"Lieutenant Edwards here, sir. Are we still friends?"

Fortunately, the Colonel laughed. "How are you doing, Dave?"

"Fine, sir, but I'm wanting to get back to flying. Do I still have a job?"

"Well, if you'll just return the ejection seat, the canopy and your parachute, I'll see if we can work you in," mused the Colonel. "Seriously, Dave, my boss, the wing commander, didn't know whether to court marshal you, give you a medal, or just kick your ass. I'll bet you a trip to Lee's hoochie that it will be the last two… especially since Stars and Stripes has picked up the story and told the world. That was one of the dumbest and bravest things I have seen in my career."

"So what do I do now, sir?"

"Well, I want you back as soon as possible, but with that shoulder, you're no good to me here…so I have something else for you while it mends."

"Yes, sir. I'm listening."

"The pilot on the stretcher, Captain Stebinski, Pete tells me you two are old friends. I have talked to the hospital commander there at Tachi. He's being moved to the burn hospital at Brook Army Medical Center in San Antonio. I want you to escort him there, take care of him on the trip, and have that shoulder looked at while you are there.

"Yes, sir. I can do that, but I want to get back to flying as soon as I can."

"Yeah, I understand. Gets in your blood, doesn't it. I will have the orders cut. Keep me posted on how it's going, and get your butt back over here as soon as you're healthy. I need you back in a cockpit ASAP. Good luck."

It wasn't what Dave wanted, but he couldn't fly for a while anyhow...so why not? A couple of long plane rides, a couple of days in the land of the big BX, a decent steak and a couple of Shiner long necks. Why not? But baby sitting Stebinski? Well, it might give him time to figure what this guy is all about. Dave never disliked Stebinski. In a weird sort of fashion, he was Stebinski...or at least wanted to be. He saw a toughness in him that he wanted to emulate. Yes, this could be an interesting few days. And why not?

Med Evac flights are not necessarily built for comfort.....more for the practicality of what they were. They were designed for getting the wounded and injured back to better medical care as quickly and as safely as possible. And the men and women who flew these day after day were another kind of angel. They had their patient for less than a day, and then went back for more. But Dave was impressed how thorough and professional they were. They maintained a sterile and friendly environment for their guests and treated them with the highest respect...as heroes. Dave was a bit embarrassed to even be on board and taking up space.

Their flight took them directly from Japan to San Antonio's Kelly AFB, with a refueling stop at Elmendorf in Alaska. The Great Circle Route sometimes seems out of the way, but it is always the shortest. They also had better advantage of the jet stream on this routing. Dave had never traveled so lightly. All of his "stuff" was back at Taegu. The hospital provided him basics of a uniform and toiletries. He hit the BX for some Levis and a couple of shirts and things. He had always been pretty low maintenance.

Dave was assigned a bunk next to Stebinski. Actually, it was a litter just like the one Stebinski was strapped to. Stebinski was very quiet during the first hour of the flight, the effect of the meds used to numb the pain. They had removed the bandages covering his face but kept it heavily medicated to fight infection. The cabin was kept cool for bacterial reasons and dim so the guests could get some sleep. "Hey, plow boy. You asleep?"

"No sir. Just passing time," answered Dave.

"Could you get me something to drink…please?"

"Sure. I hear they have buttermilk in the fridge. Want some?"

"Okay. Maybe I deserved that…maybe I didn't." Dave held the cup of water while he drank through a flex straw. "Thanks, Dave. Is it okay to call you Dave?"

"That's what my friends call me. Are you my friend?"

There was a pause. "I can be your best friend or worst enemy. What do you want me to be?"

Dave smiled. This is what he liked about Stebinski. He always answered a question with a question. He must be a chess player. "Call me Dave."

"Okay, and you can call me Captain or Stebi or Charlie. What's your pleasure?"

"Who calls you Charlie?"

"Only those who really love me."

"Okay, Stebi." Another long pause. "Tell me something. Why did the Russians want you?"

"They were told what a mean son of a bitch I was and wanted a DNA sample. Are you the one who told them?"

Dave just ignored the question.

"No, it's all part of how the Russians develop their technologies. Rather than spending a large part of their GNP on R&D, they let us develop it and then steal it however they can...including stealing our pilots. There is no telling how many of our guys that we think are either POWs or dead are actually in some Russian cell. They are always a year or so behind us, but it's a lot cheaper for them. Our squadron has been using an advanced HARM anti-radar missile against the North Korean radar sites. But this is a bit different. To hide their positions, they would only turn on their emitters for a few seconds and then turn them off. We had nothing to shoot at. But Texas Instruments came out with a great improvement. As soon as they came on, drones would lock on the GPS coordinates and forward the numbers to our airborne fighters. We would launch in the blind against the GPS coordinates. It was a terribly simple solution...and very effective. Apparently, the Russians wanted to know more about it. And that's my claim to fame. What was yours?"

"Pete and I were in the Bot Squadron. We were the ones..."

"Yeah, yeah, I know. I know all about you guys. They sent you out to war with your baby-sitter on your wing to take care of you. Was it true that your call sign was Nanny?" Stebi put his hand over his mouth to simulate an oxygen mask and mumbled, 'Tower, my nanny and I are ready for take-off.'"

Dave was both amused and pissed. But this is what he loved about Stebi. You could never get one up on him. He was clever and quick-witted. But it still pissed Dave off. And Dave only wished he could be so clever. He wasn't about to let this conversation dwindle.

"Tell me. Did you ever figure who set your napkin on fire?"

"Tell me why that's important for me to know," Stebinski countered again, every offensive move met with an equally offensive move. Dave smiled.

"Hey, Stebi. Did you go to elementary school, or did you just start with the Academy?"

"I am going to assume that you are going somewhere with that dim-witted question."

"Did you ever read a book called The Little Prince?

"Do you mean The Prince by Machiavelli? He and Attila the Hun were my childhood heroes."

"Why am I not surprised? No, this was by Antoine de Saint Exupery, a pilot like you and me."

"There ain't no pilots like you and me, Dave."

Dave thought to himself, "Was that a compliment?" Dave ignored the obvious response and paused for effect. "Well, he's dead, and we're only half dead...so far."

"So tell me about this little fairy prince and the dead pilot. Go on."

"There is a boy, the little prince, and a fox. They're having a conversation. The fox wants the boy to tame him. To make a long story short, the fox tells the boy that he must become responsible for whatever he tames. If the boy tames the fox, he will become responsible for the fox, for he changes the fox forever. The boy had already tamed a wild rose and is now responsible for the rose, its water, protection from the elements and all. Are you the fox, Stebi? Wanting to be tamed but not really wanting to be tamed because you don't want anyone to be responsible for you?"

"Or is it the other way around, Davey? The way I see it is that you saved my life. You didn't have to do that? Or maybe you did. I don't know. You couldn't just let me die. When you found out who was under these bandages, were you sorry you went to the trouble? I didn't choose to let you save me...you just did it... because that's now the way you are wired up. So when you decided to save me, you chose to become responsible for me. You tamed me. You changed me. And now you are responsible for me. Life sucks sometimes, doesn't it?"

"And another thing the fox said," Stebi continued. "It is the time you wasted on your rose that makes your rose so important. I am your rose. You and I will be connected the rest of our lives in a way that few will understand. Exupery went on to say, 'It is only with the heart that one can see; what is essential is invisible to the eye.' Neither of us will ever be able to explain our relationship…not even to ourselves. I actually became responsible for you six years ago when you were a Doolie. I tamed you, I changed you and became forever responsible for you. And I personally think I did a pretty damned good job. A lesser man would have left your buddy, Pete, in prison and I'd be in a Russian cell. Think about it."

"Sounds to me like you have read my book," questioned Dave.

"Never said I didn't. Never said I did. So what's the point of this conversation, Davey?"

"I guess I'm just trying to understand you, Stebi. Because in understanding you, I'll better understand myself."

"Isn't it strange, Dave. Here I am, a guy that you have hated for so long, and now you are discovering that we are so much alike. Scary, isn't it?"

"I never said I hated you. Do you need for me to hate you?" Dave was getting the jest of answering a question with a question. "Edwards, take a note to self," he muttered.

"That's for you to work out, Dave." Stebi had just thrown the ball back in Dave's court. He was good.

There was a long silence that Stebinski finally broke. "Dave, there's more to your story that we need to cover before I fall asleep. I can feel the drugs working on my brain. You said that the fox wanted to be tamed. Why did the fox want to be tamed? Why do we want to be tamed? Why do we put ourselves in a position to be tamed? Why did you come to the Academy? Why do we open ourselves up to a friendship, like you and Pete Benedetto? Why do we fall in love? Why did I get married? Why do we love and fear God at the same time? It's all about wanting to be tamed...just like the fox. Davey, I am the fox. You are the fox in this story."

"I came to the Academy to become a man, to grow strong and independent, to get a great education that would carry me through life, to have a career."

"So when Dave Edwards came to the Air Force Academy, it was all about Dave Edwards. Right?"

"Well, I never thought of it that way. I guess that's true."

"That's bullshit, plow boy. I'm guessing you were pretty much a loner growing up, and you made the decision to let someone tame you when you came to the Academy. You were looking for something, and you knew that you would need to allow yourself to be tamed to get it. Am I getting too close?"

Stebi could tell from Dave's silence that he was in the core of Dave's soul and continued. "Don't consider being tough inconsistent with being a good person...a good friend. I grew up on the streets. I had to be tough to survive. It's who I am. But don't think for a minute that I'm not capable of loving, of caring, of being loved...or reading your cute little book. You gotta see it, Dave. We are more alike than we are different."

Stebi continued. "It comes down to this, Dave. We all want to be tamed. The fox wanted it. The rose in the story wanted it. If we are mentally sound, we want to be tamed and be a part of the fellowship of man. We want to have free choice in our lives, but we also want to be a cog in this wheel, part of the Long Blue Line. Listen. I got the world's greatest wife waiting for me back in the States. When I got shot down, my first thought was of her and how I let her down. By agreeing to be married, we each allowed ourselves to be tamed by the other. I became responsible for her, and she became responsible for me. That's what a good marriage is all about. When I got shot down, I let down my end of the deal. I am going to get healed up and healthy again so I can be part of this partnership again."

"So let me carry this one step deeper, Davey. I know the meds are kicking in, but I want to get this out. I don't know what your relationship with God is, but check out the similarities. Sure, I need God in my life, and he's there for me. I fear Him, and I love Him. He loves me, but He doesn't fear me. He fears losing me. You see, He needs me just as much as I need Him. Likewise, I need my wife just as much as she needs me. That's why I'm a tough guy…and strong and smart and caring…because I want and need to be in relationships. I need to be tamed…and I am willing to do my part." Stebi took a deep breath and paused as he thought about how far to carry this. "And I need you as much as you need me…and that, my friend, is the Law of the Jungle."

Dave was speechless. Stebi had bored a hole in his soul and walked right in. He hadn't invited him, he just did it. Stebi was tough enough to allow himself to be tamed. He was man enough to love and be loved. He was the answer to Dave's many questions about his own life.

Dave sat there long after Stebi had fallen asleep, thinking on their discussion. It was dark outside and dim and quiet inside the Med Evac. Dave felt at home in the air. He was among his comrades, his warriors, and loved them one and all. He was proud to be part of this and proud to be tamed. But he was proudest of his new friend, Charlie Stebinski.

* * *

27

The Med Evac wasn't long on the ground at Elmendorf...just long enough to refuel and change flight crew members. For safety reasons, everyone needed to at least be awake during refueling. One could leave the aircraft if they chose, but they needed to remain in the immediate area for this quick turn-around. Dave had never been to Alaska, so he got off just to say he'd been there. Even though it was five in the afternoon, it was very dark, a typical winter day for this northern tier base. The Northern Lights were filing the skies, dancing around like a pink curtain in a wind storm. He guessed this was pretty common for the locals since the ground crew prepping the airplane hardly seemed to notice. Dave couldn't take his eyes off this phenomenon. Once in Montana during a period of extreme sun burst activity, he had sampled the Northern Lights, but nothing like this.

The airplane was soon ready for re-boarding so he grabbed a bag of moose jerky from the BX kiosk for Stebi. He questioned why he did that, then he questioned why he questioned. "This is just what friends do," Dave mused.

Without speaking, Dave took his place next to Stebi, ripped open the jerky and placed the bag on his chest within reach of his good hand. "Okay, what the hell is this?"

"I found something tougher than you are, Stebi."

"Hmmmf. I doubt it." But he took a piece, and then another. "Thanks, buddy." Stebi rolled over to look out the small window into the cold darkness. The Northern Lights had quieted down. Dave took that as his not wanting to talk any more…and he was right. He had other things on his mind.

Somewhere over the Canadian Rockies, Stebi broke his silence. "Dave, you awake?"

"Yeah…more or less. What's up?"

"Davey, the clock's running out on me…and I hate to admit it, but I'm more than just a little scared."

"What the hell are you talking about, Stebi. You're not dying from these injuries. You're going to be fine."

"Actually, dying might be easier. You see, at the end of this flight, I gotta face someone, and she means all the world to me…more than life itself."

"You'd better be talking about your wife."

"I am, you moron. Never mind. I knew I shouldn't have brought it up."

"Talk to me, Charlie. What's going on?"

"Look at me, Davey. I'm all beat up…useless. And my face is burned to a crisp."

"Is that what this is all about? You're afraid your wife won't love you if your face is scarred? I don't know much about women…well, wives. I've never been in that serious of a relationship with a girl. But listening to you earlier, I figure she fell in love with all of you…not just your handsome face and Charles Atlas body. For you to think any less doesn't say much for your wife."

"Davey, she's an angel. I couldn't ask for a better wife or a better person. She completes me. She makes me want to be a better person. She has tamed me…no doubt. And I love it."

"Well, let me reverse it. What if she were in an accident and scarred? What if she had cancer and had to have a breast removed? What if some day she grows old? You would be right there by her side loving every inch of her…and she'll do the same. You're no coward. I know that. But you are doing the coward thing…dying a thousand times. You'll know the minute you see her how much she loves you and will love you. You will see it in her eyes and feel it in her touch. That's what love is all about. She loves all of you…regardless. But because she loves you, she's part of you, and she'll hurt with you… and you gotta let her. You two will get through this thing together…and that will strengthen your relationship."

"How do you know so much about love, Davey? You told me that you have never been in a serious relationship. Have you ever been in love?"

"I thought I was once. I met this girl back in the Springs…"

"And?"

"I never called her back."

"Talk about being a coward."

"Yeah, and I still think about her all the time."

"Well, Davey. You ought to do something about it. Take some action. It's better to have loved and lost than never to have loved at all. Shakespeare, I think."

"Maybe, someday."

"Yeah, right. You big pussy."

The rest of the flight into San Antonio was quiet and smooth. When they deplaned at Kelly AFB, the ambulatory patients like Dave boarded a bus while ambulances carried the litter patients to the center at Brooks. "I'll come by and check on you tomorrow, Stebi. Good luck…and remember, the doctors know more about it than you do." Stebi waved good bye with the social finger of his good hand.

* * *

28

After his initial examination, Dave was posted as an out-patient and given a room in the guest officers' quarters across the street from the hospital. He was given an appointment to see a specialist the following afternoon. It was a cool winter's day in San Antonio, a good day to take a walk and clear the clouds from his mind. His life had been crazy this past week and he needed time to reload, reflect and just relax. As he left his room, he looked across at the big hospital and decided to visit his buddy…after his walk.

Stebinski was given an immediate full exam upon his arrival. The broken arm had been set properly, and there was nothing they could do for it other than let time heal the bone. The burns on his leg were more serious than those on his face, fortunately, and those, too, would heal with time. Scarring might be an issue, but not a big issue. Stebi was happy with that news.

Once the treatment was completed, the attending nurse put her hand on his arm. "I have the best medicine in the world for you now, Captain. Your wife is in the waiting room. Are you ready to see her?"

His heart was racing. "Can you put a bandage or something over the side of my face? I don't want to scare her."

"No," she said…with all the love of a drill sergeant. "You look fine, Captain. Stop worrying about it. I'll go get her. She really wants to see you."

As his wife entered the room, Stebi saw her in a new light. He realized that, indeed, he loved every inch of her, just as Dave had said. He would love her regardless and forever. She was his mate. She paused just for a moment and looked on Stebi with a love that had always been there but he had perhaps never noticed. He knew Dave was right.

She came to his side, held his hand to her chest, and tears began to fill her eyes. 'Charlie, I thought I had lost you. I'm so happy you came back to me. Now scoot over." She crawled up in the hospital bed and cuddled up next to him. He put his good arm around her and said a short prayer, thanking God for good women. It was just then that Dave, seeing the two on the bed, knocked on the door and entered the room.

"Dave, I want you to meet my wife, Dawn. You probably feel that you already know her…from all the talking we did on the airplane."

Dave just stood in the doorway, stunned, with his mouth open. Dawn broke the pregnant moment. She went over to Dave and gave him an open hug.

"I understand you are the guy who saved my husband's life. Thank you. Thank you. Thank you."

For the next fifteen or twenty minutes, the three of them just made small talk, but Dave was not really in the conversation. He couldn't take his eyes off Dawn. "Davey, you seem to be a million miles away. Are you okay?"

"Yeah, Stebi. They have me on some meds, and I'm kinda zoned out. Glad I'm not flying today."

A nurse entered the room. "I need to change Captain Stebinski's dressings and clean him up. Can you two leave the room for a while? There is a waiting room just down the hallway."

"Why don't you two go get some breakfast," suggested Stebinski. "Surely, they have a snack bar somewhere here in this joint."

"Uh huh," Dave mumbled and headed for the door.

As the elevator doors shut behind them, Dawn turned to Dave without speaking and gave him a kiss like the one he had always dreamed of…but not in this circumstance. Her lips were as full and soft as he'd expected. "Thanks, Dave."

"No. Thank you."

"I meant for bringing Charlie back."

They were both quiet as they got their coffee and sat down on the outside patio. The warmth of the sun felt good on this cool south Texas day. "This is a little awkward, Dawn. I had no idea that Stebi was your Charlie."

"I didn't know that you were my hero until you just walked into his room."

"Dawn, you don't know how much I have thought about you since that day at the truck stop. I still carry that piece of paper with your lipstick. It still has a bit of your fragrance on it." Dawn could feel herself blushing a bit. "I don't know why, but every girl I have been with since, I always compare them with you. Maybe that's why I can't seem to have a serious relationship."

"So how come you never called…or anything? I wanted you to."

Dave paused before he answered. "I thought you were off the market…with Charlie. That's what you told me."

"I wanted you to call."

"I honestly have thought about you every day since I met you." Dave questioned how far to go with this, but couldn't help but continue. "Dawn, I have loved you ever since I met you." There, he had said it.

"So where do we go from here?"

"Do you love Charlie?"

"Charlie loves me. He takes such good care of me. He treats me like a lady. He opens the door for me. He wants me to have dreams and goals…and helps me chase them. He wants me to be proud of him and proud of myself. You guys see another side of Charlie than I do. He is soft and gentle and caring."

"You didn't say you loved him."

"Dave, when I heard he had been shot down, part of me died. Then they told me he'd been taken as a prisoner, not a minute went by that I didn't think about him, about what he was doing at that moment, wondering if he were thinking about me. I was there with him…wherever he was…every minute of every day. Then I heard he was rescued, but badly injured. I promised to God that if He returned just a part of him back to me, I would love him and care for him. I discovered then just how I really felt. Do I love Charlie Stebinski? You bet your sweet ass I do…like the sun coming up in the morning, like the gentle rain, like the heat of the roaring campfire. I more than love my husband: I like him. I trust him to always have me in his heart. And I will always be so thankful to you for bringing him back."

Dave pondered on Dawn's declaration for a few moments as she sipped her coffee and watched for Dave's response. He arose and walked over to her chair, bent down and kissed her on the cheek…and whispered in her ear, "I will always love you."

"No, Dave. You're not in love with me. You're in love with a dream. You're in love with being in love. We spent maybe an hour together back at that truck stop in Colorado Springs. That's all. Sure, there was some chemistry. I felt it, and I think you did, too. But you never followed up on it. You can pretend to be in love with me, but you cannot pretend to be there for me…

and you weren't. Charlie was…and always has been. He spent his time on me and with me. That's just how love works, Dave."

"And one more thing, Dave. And I haven't even told Charlie this yet. I was about to tell him when you walked into his room. We were going to wait until this awful war was over before starting a family. Charlie refused to leave a widow with a child. But late last summer, we met in Hawaii for R&R. Well, we have a little boy on the way."

With that, Dave walked slowly to the edge of the patio, turned and blew Dawn a kiss, and returned to his room across the street. His whole world had tumbled. He picked up the phone and called the MAC Flight Terminal. "Got any flights going west today?'

"How far west?"

"Korea."

"Yessir, got a C-5 going to Hawaii and then on to Yokota Air Force Base, Japan. Shouldn't be any problem getting a hop on over to Korea from there. Leaves in two hours. Want on it?"

"Yes. Lieutenant David Edwards, combat priority. One seat, please."

* * *

29

The C-5 is a huge airplane. To see one in the traffic pattern is like seeing a hangar fly by. They look incredibly slow because they are so large, but they can carry big stuff and heavy stuff all around the world...very quickly. Dave climbed the ladder into the passenger compartment high up in the tail section...a difficult feat with one arm in a sling. 'What's the load today, Sergeant?" Dave asked of the Loadmaster. He really didn't care...just making conversation.

"20mm ammo, several jet engines, a couple of those new robot planes and 40 pallets of beer, sir."

Dave found a seat. They were very large seats, designed for delivering a combat-ready soldier anywhere in the world. There was plenty of room surrounding the seats for combat gear. Dave was still traveling light and half asleep by the time the wheels were up.

It had been one hell of a week for Dave. He had lost his best friend, and then he saved him. He had bailed out of a perfectly good airplane and then botched the landing. He had seen the business end of a bunch of bayonets and the inside of a bamboo cell. He had taken a ride in a Russian chopper, played Russian roulette with a hand grenade and had killed two of its crew. He had run from the North Koreans, the Chinese and the Russians in a stolen helicopter, played cat and mouse with the US Navy and actually landed on one of their boats. He had met the real Charlie Stebinski, the real Dawn whatever her last name was, and perhaps finally, the real Dave Edwards…or perhaps not.

Dave had lots of time for reflection circling the globe back to Korea. What was he really all about? Where was he going? Where was he now? He had learned a great deal about himself…especially from his discussions with Stebi.

Probably the most important thing he learned from his new friend was why he was like he was…especially as a cadet. Stebi was always hard on Dave and Pete. He could always determine just how far they could go and then would push them just a little farther. He was the reason they had been so successful at the Zoo. He was the reason they had grown so much. And Dave now realized that Stebi was that way for two reasons. First, he loved the Academy and what it had done for him. He recognized that and wanted to do what was best for the Academy and its cadets. Secondly, he loved Pete and Dave…and saw a lot of himself in them. He wanted them to be just a strong and as tough as he. And he wanted them to get the most and the best of what the Academy offered.

Stebi just inherited Pete and Dave…or was it a God thing? Did fate bring them together, or was Stebi just another of God's many blessings salted into their lives? What would their lives be like if Stebi had not entered and then re-entered their lives?

Sure, Stebi was a tough guy, but as Dawn had pointed out and as Dave could now so easily recognize, he was both tough and gentle. The gentle side is what Dawn loved and Dave coveted. The tough side is what allowed Dawn to feel safe and what Dave already shared…but not with the accompanying wisdom.

Dave knew Stebi would make a great father when that time came. Likewise, he hoped he would be a great father…but questioned if he would ever get that far in life. Certainly, Dave learned a lot about himself, but the most valuable lesson was that he discovered he really did not know himself well enough…at least not as well as he had thought. A lot of questions were answered, but more were generated.

Dave couldn't wait to get back to Taegu, back to flying and especially back to his buddy, Pete. He had so much to tell Pete…about his talks with Stebi and about his encounter with Dawn…and about his own discoveries about himself. The flying would help ease the mind and get him started again on a new life…a life with Stebi in it and Dawn out of it. He mulled over these many thoughts and questions and discoveries as the C-5 sped him back toward his life in Korea.

"What a week it has been," Dave spoke out loud. "I wonder if Dawn has a sister."

* * *

30

As the C-5 rolled out on final approach at Yokota in Japan, Pete was just breaking ground with his robotic wingman across the Sea of Japan at Taegu. He hadn't heard from Dave since he left Japan for San Antonio and figured he was just enjoying the time off. Pete had gone through pilot training at Randolph AFB in San Antonio and had learned to love that city. It had all the class and charm that Philly and Baltimore and DC and the rest of his right coast haunts could only hope for. He would have suggested several good places there if he had had the time before Dave departed…places like Earl Abel's, the Auger Inn and Casa Rio. Oh, and the Ratskeller at Fort Sam. He missed his buddy.

Ming, Pete's robotic wingman, had already moved into fingertip formation position on his right wing and was talking via secure data link with R2, Pete's on-board computer. They were receiving intel from squadron planes returning from the combat area. Pete missed his old airplane, #6400, but it was splattered on a mountainside up north. Pete's chute still hung in the tree tops there. He was glad to have all of that behind him and realized he really had not thanked Dave for his rescue and his bravery. He vowed to take care of that at the first opportunity in proper fashion.

Today's mission was another search-and-destroy, shoot anything that moves mission. Electronic sensors hanging in the jungle canopy had picked up both ignition signals and audio suggesting there was a large convoy of Chinese-built trucks moving south on Route 9 between choke points 3 and 5. A choke point is a tight area, such as a mountain pass or a narrow valley where all traffic must pass. Areas around a choke point were kept pretty well bombed out so traffic through these areas could be seen easily. The trucks could be identified from their unique ignition patterns and the sound patterns of their exhausts. It was their fingerprint. The ignition pattern even gave them a clue to how heavily loaded it was…how hard it would struggle to get up a particular hill or such. This was Artificial Intelligence at its best.

Pete sent Ming down to check for truck traffic and AAA response. These large convoys usually carried along their own truck-mounted AAA. He did draw fire but got a visual on the convoy and marked it with a flare. Pete rolled in just as he got a visual of a missile coming up from the convoy's location. All missile warnings triggered simultaneously, and jamming and flares began. Ming was about a mile away readying for another strafing attack and could not help Pete. The auto jammer fooled the missile into exploding about 100 meters before it got to Pete, but the shrapnel still impacted Pete's plane on the right wing. The plane shuddered hard but was controllable. Pete's visual of holes in his wing were validated by the automatic skin sensors, and the strain gauges on the wing spars verified significant damage.

Pete pulled off the target and strained for altitude while R2 performed a systems check on the fighter. Ming had returned to fingertip position and relayed a picture to Pete showing his airplane with the right landing gear partially extended, a result of the missile damage. Pete responded with the traditional, "Oh shit!" And just then, a bad day quickly got worse.

"MiG alert" was the call over the emergency channel that the communicator expert system would pass immediately to the pilot regardless of the mission situation. Most calls were delayed if the pilot were in a high stress portion of the mission, but the pilot himself could customize this feature to fit his own capabilities and desires as to what messages were held for later playback and what messages were simply trashed. The entire combat zone was saturated with radar coverage and anytime the MiGs came up to play, they not only were noticed, but became prime targets for allied pilots in quest of being an Ace...and that included Pete. No real pilot would pass the chance to paint that red star on the side of his cockpit. The question had never been answered as to who got credit for the kill if the robot shot down the MiG.

Air superiority had been a fact of the entire war for the Allies, both in quantity and quality, so the MiGs would only come up when they had a distinct advantage, such as marginal weather or light allied fighter cover. Pete knew conditions were prime today but wanted no part of a MiG because of his sick airframe. He was not to have his way.

As Pete climbed through a light shower with his pitot tube pointed at the home drome, a MiG alert was sounded for the Valley Highway area. The MiGs would stay down below the ceiling where maneuverability was limited and down low in the valley to shield themselves from radar coverage. Normally, they appeared single-ship, for they had to stay as maneuverable as possible in the mountains and came with the intent of hit-and-run, not sustained air-to-air engagements. Such tactics had proven very successful for them two days earlier when a single MiG attacked a helicopter rescue effort, downing both choppers, who had been forced to work below the overcast with no fighter cover. The enemy was very clever in employing their limited fighter resources only when they perceived their local air superiority.

Ming and R2 simultaneously painted an unknown Bogie and due to the MiG alert coupled with the flight characteristics gave it a high probability of being a Bandit, a MiG. It was not emitting as far as R2's scanners could perceive but was approaching the flight in a threatening manner. There was little Pete could do with his damaged aircraft to evade, so he called Ming into close trail position. Since the MiG was not using his radar and was approaching through his optimum missile range, and since the enemy was somewhat short of air-to-air missiles due to resupply problems, R2 deduced and notified Pete of the high probability of a cannon pass. R2 recommended a slash-back-split defensive maneuver where both aircraft performed a hard-as-possible descending turn in opposite directions. Since Pete was at a fairly low airspeed that would decrease in the hard turn and since he was at a low altitude, he quickly reconnected his zero-delay lanyard to give him an instant opening parachute should this situation not work out. Even if the MiG did not get him, he feared that damaged wing might fold up under the high g loading of a max performance turn. On the mark, Pete broke hard left while Ming broke right. The MiG driver chose to turn with the wrong target, Pete, for in the Commie's mind, it was a more lucrative target and no real fighter pilot brags at the bar over shooting down a drone. Anyhow, the drone would be easy prey, he figured, with the master gone.

It took Ming mere seconds at 20 g's to turn behind the MiG, whose attention was turned fully on Pete. Ming had turned so quickly, however, that he was too close to deploy a missile. The three were in close trail with the MiG firing on Pete and Ming waiting until he had a picture of the MiG without Pete in it so he could fire. Pete was limited in his maneuverability due to his damage and could not shake the MiG. R2 sensed the additional damage being dealt to Pete's aircraft by the MiG's cannon and commanded Ming to commence firing regardless.

With Ming's tremendous maneuverability coupled with his computer-aimed cannon, the MiG was short lived. Ming fired only 150 rounds, a two-second burst, that impacted the MiG in the left wing root, taking out the main spar, separating the left wing from the fuselage. The MiG exploded, spreading flaming debris into the jungle below.

Several of Ming's cannon rounds passed by and through the MiG, through Pete's airplane. One round ripped off Pete's right shoulder and shattered his spine, setting fire to his oxygen-rich mask and flight helmet. Another round hit Pete in the hip and shattered his pelvis. Pete never felt the pain.

Pete's plane and Ming remained airworthy throughout the encounter. R2 was performing the built-in-test program for battle damage assessment and monitoring Pete's failing vital signs as Ming picked up R2's damaged functions. When R2 deemed Pete incapable of aircraft control, he notified Pete of his intent to take control of the aircraft and did so when Pete failed to respond. R2 set course for home and updated the Ops computer of the situation. The flight home was uneventful with R2 and Ming monitoring systems performance and adjusting.

The standard recovery involved an ILS approach and landing, but conditions were far from standard with R2's battle damage reducing the probability of a safe landing without Pete to less than fifty percent. On a better day, Pete had programmed R2 for such a contingency. R2 lined up to fly down the runway at a thousand feet, and when about mid-field, Pete's lifeless body was ejected from the cockpit. In the event R2 might crash before landing, Pete had made other plans for his remains.

As R2 directed the empty airplane back to a landing, Pete's shattered body drifted down slowly beneath the shredded drab nylon canopy, another number, another flag. Death comes quickly and slowly, continuously. But always it comes.

* * *

Epitaph ···

The howling winds once again owned Stanley Canyon.
The snow flakes were so large Dave could almost hear
them crashing down through the aspen branches and
hitting the rocks. The light from his lantern reached
into the darkness, creating ominous living shadows
from the swaying pines and aspens, yet the spirits were
content.

From his backpack Dave pulled a dark green bottle
of red wine and a brass canister wrapped in solemn
velvet. Dave filled two glasses and raised his in silent
salute against the wind. He threw his emptied glass
into the rocky canyon below, for he would need it no
more. He spread the ashes in the canister onto the
velvet at the base of the second glass, and soon they
succumbed to the swirling winds.

In accordance with Pete's wishes, his ashes were being
returned to the mountains, his home. As they were
carried away piece by piece, Dave knelt in the fresh
powdery snow and prayed that Pete had finally found
his peace and that his soul was already secure in God's
heaven. He missed his friend. The love between them
was unending even in death.

Dave reopened the envelope that Pete had left for him
and read it again one last time:

This is not the end, my foolish friend,
For mine is an empty grave.
So try not to cry nor bid me good-bye.
Become not the grim reaper's slave.

I choose not to hold that billet so cold.
I reject that intolerable state.
Though I know Master's law, I ignore His call,
For my spirit He must patiently wait.

The key He has given to me for His heaven,
A place to His right I do pray.
Yet when He showed me the worth of His heaven on earth,
He gave me the reason to stay.

So look for me in the evening sunset,
In the twinkle of the morning star.
I polish the stone in the mountain stream.
I erase all evidence of war.

I share my strength with the mountain range.
I bend with the evergreen.
He allows me to guide the on-rushing tide.
He has granted me respite supreme.

I am as close to you as the morning dew,
As the smell of the freshly-cut hay,
The sound of night of the hoot owl in flight,
The crush of the snow 'neath the sleigh.

Through nature I roam, my most heavenly home.
I serve at my Master's grace.
Tho' the body is done, my spirit lives on.
He has given me paths to retrace.

So try not to cry nor bid me good-bye,
For this happiness someday you'll share.

When your time is through, I will be waiting for you,
And for you a place I prepare.

From the pocket of his old canvas pack, Dave took out
his orange-handled switchblade knife, the kind issued
to pilots to carry in the thigh pocket of their flight suit.
Very carefully he worked at the threads securing the
bulldog patch to the pack until it came loose.

As in the oriental custom, Dave wrapped Pete's epitaph
around an aspen branch and wrapped the old patch
around that, securing it with a piece of shroud line he
had cut from the pack. He stood to attention, and in
the now sacred canyon feeling very much alone, Dave
muttered the words of the chorus of the Air Force
song:

Here's a toast to the host of those who love the vastness
of the sky,
To a friend we will send the message of his brother
men who fly.
We drink to those who gave their all of old,
Then down we dive to score the rainbow's pot of
gold.
A toast to the host of the men we boast,
The U.S. Air Force.

Dave rendered his friend a final salute and quietly
started back down the trail.

Surely the howling winds of Stanley Canyon have long
ago carried the message away, just as they dispersed
Pete's ashes. But the thought and spirit live eternally
there in Stanley Canyon as anyone can tell you who has
trespassed on a cold and snowy night.

And again, as fellow airman Antoine de Saint Exupery wrote in the year of Pete's birth:

> "It is only with the heart that one can see rightly;
> What is essential is invisible to the eye."

And that, my friend, is truly the Law of the Jungle.

* * *